About the Author

Before finally deciding to write her first Young Adult novel, Debra was a hair and make-up artist. Two of Debra's most memorable experiences as a hair and make-up artist were having the honour of assisting the Bafta nominated make-up artist Wally Schneiderman (The Elephant Man, Labyrinth, Chaplin) and his daughter Beryl Lerman (Braveheart, Yentl) in their workshops; and the learning curve that was working three summers at the upstate New York prestigious performing arts camp 'Stagedoor Manor'.

Throughout Debra's make-up career she always found

herself working with children, occasionally being the make-up artist for the packaging of the Crayola products or, being assigned to the child actors on productions.

After eleven years of being in the hair and make-up artist industry, Debra decided she wanted a change. Not knowing exactly what she wanted to do, she decided to study various courses including: Event Management, Set Design for TV & Film, and Acting for TV & Film at the New York Film Academy—leading her to live in Brooklyn, above a laundrette (how cliche!) for six months. After studying in NYC, Debra decided to dig out an old feature film screenplay she had written, take out a couple of the scenes and put together a sample. From that, Debra then went onto cast, direct, and produce.

Debra thoroughly enjoyed the casting process and made the decision to include her enjoyment of the casting process with her enjoyment of working with, and looking after, child actors and applied for a chaperone license, that was in 2013. Since 2013 Debra has chaperoned on various West End productions such as 'Charlie and the Chocolate Factory', 'Annie', and 'Matilda the Musical'. Debra also had the opportunity to combine her Event Management, Acting for TV & Film' and experience working with children between the ages of seven and eighteen together and spending one Summer at the other upstate New York prestigious performing arts camp 'French Woods Festival' in their production office, assisting in their charity events, birthday parties and the Children's self-tape auditions that were then sent to leading casting directors within the TV & Film industry.

As well as her love of writing, and chaperoning, Debra is also a Reiki two practitioner, and currently training to become a child counsellor.

The Nephilim Guard

Dearest Victoria,

Your Support, and kindness
has been immense.

Thank you!

All My love
Debra x x x

Debra Cohen

The Nephilim Guard

Olympia Publishers
London

www.olympiapublishers.com
OLYMPIA PAPERBACK EDITION

A CIP catalogue record for this title is
available from the British Library.

ISBN: 978-1-80074-488-2

Names and Characters except the reference to the Greek Gods and
Goddesses and the brief mentions of the names Stefan Zgrzembski
and Irena Sendler are the author's imagination. Any resemblance to
actual persons, living or dead is purely coincidental.

First Published in 2023

Olympia Publishers
Tallis House
2 Tallis Street
London
EC4Y 0AB

Printed in Great Britain

Dedication

For Mum, Dad and Kerry-Anne. Thank you for your continuous support , acceptance, and encouragement. I am eternally grateful.

Chapter One

Warsaw, 1939.

"I was taught since my earliest years that people are either good or bad. Their race, nationality, and religion do not matter, what matters is the person."

This was a quote Irena's father once told her. As she had grown older, she had come to realise that he was right, mostly. She had come to discover that no one is bad, it is just they have made choices which they felt were right for them but had led others to an experience of suffering. But we cannot blame them for making those choices, for those decisions were based upon their own personal truths and what is the truth for you, may not be the truth for another; that does not necessarily make their truths wrong. Although suffering is of course tragic, Irena had learnt that without suffering, there would be no compassion, just like to discover what we want, first we must experience what we do not want.

"Irena!"

Irena woke from her contemplative state to turn and face the lady who shouted out her name.

"Lena." Irena embraced her mousey-haired friend, and kissed each other on either cheek in welcome.

"Irena, Earnest and I are having a dinner gathering tomorrow night, you should come. He has invited a gentleman, a colleague of his, very handsome, a fellow lawyer named

Stefan. He seems a kind man. I think you two would be very compatible." Irena looks at her beloved friend. She was always trying to set her up with random men.

"Lena, I appreciate you trying to find a man for me, but I have already told you, I am not wanting a relationship at this time."

Irena takes in the dark, grey, dull streets of Warsaw that surround them. Streets full of vagrant children, and men, mostly tradesmen, dressed in work shirts and dungarees, or overalls in colours of beige, and grey.

"Irena, you say you would like to have children, you cannot do that without a man, you're not getting any younger. We are not like men; women have time limits."

"I am perfectly aware that we have time limits, but you know how I feel. Now is not the time to be thinking of bringing a child into the world. Hard times are approaching, and fast."

Irena stops walking, turning to face her friend, placing a gentle hand under her elbow. "There are rumours. The Nazi's are making their way into Poland, recruiting soldiers, weeding out the Jews. We have to be careful." A perturbed look crosses Lena's face.

"I understand your concern, but, Irena, we have to still try to live our lives the best we are able too. Please come tomorrow night?" With a sigh, Irena looks at her dear, loyal friend with her cool blue eyes.

"Okay, but please do not get your hopes up. I will meet Stefan, but with friendship in mind only."

*

Irena approaches a tall, white building. Cracks, and crumbling

10

stone show in various places. As she enters through the main door, she looks up at the old wooden staircase running through the apartment block. The walls which were once painted white, have greyed, have damp stains and running cracks all over them. Dressed in a white blouse, and a black skirt that ends mid-shin, her hair in plaits, pinned to the top of her head, she starts to make her way up the stairs. She reaches a rectangular wooden door, and knocks. A moment later Lena opens the door, wearing a Navy coloured tea dress. Her mousy hair was braided, some strands of hair had come loose and were framing her small heart shaped face, and she was cradling a baby in her arms. Lena kisses Irena's cheek. As Irena enters further into the apartment, Lena stops her.

"Irena, Stefan didn't come alone." Irena follows Lena into the dining area. Around the table she sees Lena's husband, Earnest, a lanky man, with bright copper hair, and freckles. Sat next to him, a broad shouldered, dark-haired man, with a tawny complexion, and strong features; Lena was right, he is handsome. Next to him, sat a lady, strikingly beautiful, her hair golden with hints of copper tones. Irena thought her skin resembled marble. Earnest stood; the other guests followed as Earnest introduced them.

"Irena Sendler, meet Stefan Zgrzembski and Miss Celestyna Zaborski." Irena gives them a smile and a nod. Stefan returning the smile, catches Irena off guard. It was a smile that held warmth and kindness.

"Miss Sendler, it is a pleasure to finally meet you, I have heard so much about you."

*

Mount Olympus, the year: 1499

In the centre of a grand room, panelled with gold flooring, and six white marble columns standing on either side of the grand hall, stands an older man wearing a white tailored suit. His hair is white, with a matching white beard: neatly trimmed surrounding his mouth, jaw, and chin. In front of him,
stands a large oval shaped glass window, placed on top of a stone statue of a hand clutching a lightning bolt. A lady with honey blonde hair, styled in a fashionable bob, wearing a white suit, enters the grand room to join him.

"Father," the woman says, her voice smooth, and warm. The man turns, facing his daughter, who continues to walk towards him.

"Athena, I need your astuteness regarding a situation that is arising on Earth's plane."

Athena peers into the window, a crease appears between her brows, as her eyes narrow.

"But what is it?" Zeus looks down at her, then back through the window.

"The mortals that carry our blood, their abilities have remained dormant, but now, since the shift, they have started to wake. I see a great danger coming, someone, or something is going to try and change their history and put an end to the Nephilim race. Athena as you know, if it is achieved, the Sky Gods will not be happy, they will attempt to extinguish them. If they do, I am not sure the gods will be able to help them again. Our strength was greatly weakened after the last great war for Earth." Zeus voice is filled with apprehension. Athena looks at her father,

"We cannot allow that to happen. I advise that you call for the others, send us to Earth, distribute us. We must recruit as many Nephilim as we can, train them to control their abilities. If you see someone, or something approaching with the goal to change history, and destroy the Nephilim, the chances are they will attempt to gather others to join in on their crusade. Once on Earth, we will be able to investigate further, and take whatever precautions, actions necessary." Zeus places his arm around his daughter's shoulders.

"Athena, do you think that is wise? To send you all back to the mortal plane? So much has changed since our last visit."

"Father, you wanted my wisdom, this is the solution I see. Send us to them, there we will be able to recruit the Nephilim, prepare, and gather troops; take whatever actions that are required. What you see, may not manifest, but if it does, it is better to be prepared."

*

Salisbury, the year: 2048

A comely young lady with long auburn hair tied into a long loose braid. Her skin possessing a warm, sun kissed tone, is exploring a large stone structure. Around her, other students are exploring the structure also. The girl's name is Viola, however her friends, and family always called her Lola, since that's the name she prefers. Lola has always been a strong willed, opinionated individual, who consistently found herself involved, and caught in the most incongruent situations.

How strange and unexpected life is, Viola thought as she continued to listen to her professor talk about the myths and legends that surrounded the mysterious origins of the large stoned structure that is Stonehenge. Tracing the stones with her fingers, they felt warm, welcoming, and smooth against her touch.

"Lola!" a fellow student calls to her, Lola turns to face the fellow student, suddenly she feels an electric bolt explode throughout her, causing her to catch her breath.

Suddenly, Lola found herself no longer standing at Stonehenge. Above her, a large stone rested horizontally on two other stones, standing vertically, and parallel to one another. In front of her, stood a large manor house. A man was walking towards her, putting on some gloves, he looks up and sees her, a look of surprise upon his face. Lola, clearly seeing him now, realises he is not a man, not a boy either, maybe eighteen or nineteen years of age. Lola felt herself stumble backwards, she reaches out to prevent herself from falling, instantaneously feeling another electric bolt occur, and then finds herself back at Stonehenge.

*

Who was that? Josiah thought, as the girl re-entered the portal dolmen at Pentre Ifan and vanished. Turning on his heels, he makes his way back to the manor, towards the library, made his way down one of the secret passageways. This passageway started behind the south facing bookshelf in the grand Victorian decor library. The library was Josiah and his unidentical twin brother Atticus's favourite room in the house; the shelves were made of mahogany and reached all the way up to a domed—stained glass—ceiling. As Josiah starts down the passageway, he pulls out a mini flashlight from his trouser pocket, illuminating his sharp features, his hazel eyes, medium-short light brown hair with copper tones, and the grey, damp stones in which the house was once originally built. Out of all the secret passages within the manor house, this one had always been the one to send chills up and down Josiah's spine. He comes to a steel door, presses his thumb against a small electronic black box (which is attached to the wall) to the side of the door. The black box flashes green, a keypad ejects from the side of the box. Josiah types in a code and the door slides open revealing a large, basic room, with tall white walls.

A large computer screen is hanging on one of the large white walls. Athena is standing in front of a black steel pedestal, on top of the pedestal is a computer keypad with various letters, symbols, numbers, and coloured buttons. On the large screen, hanging on the wall is a map of the world, on the map, hundreds of little red, yellow, and green dots are spread across it. Athena is studying the map; she turns to see Josiah walking towards her with a look of indomitability upon his face.

"A girl came through our portal," he says to her. Athena looks at Josiah. "Just now. She came through, then stumbled back through and vanished." Josiah could see worry appear upon Athena's face. "I don't think it was intentional. Going by her face she looked just as stunned as I did to find herself here."

"Were you able to get a good look at her? Do you think you would be able to recognise her if you saw a picture?" Athena asks Josiah.

"Yes, I think so," Josiah answers. Athena turns to face the image of the world map on the large computer screen hanging on the wall.

"We can run a physical description search." They both look at the large screen hanging on the tall, white wall in front of them. Athena starts to throw questions at Josiah about the mystery girl's identity.

"Age roughly?"

"Seventeen to eighteen."

"Hair colour?"

"It was in a braid, I think it was brown, or dark red, I couldn't really see."

"Height?"

"Five foot five or six."

"Skin?"

"Medium-dark Caucasian."

"Any kind of markings, a scar, a mole, eye colour?"

"She was too far away, I couldn't see," Josiah says.

Athena finishes typing in Josiah's answers, presses the yellow button on the keypad. On the screen, the red, and green dots, and a large percentage of the yellow dots vanish, leaving only a few yellow dots. Athena presses a button on the keypad, various headshots of girls, and addresses next to their photographs, appear on the large computer screen before them. Athena turns to Josiah, who is looking at the headshots; "Five hundred and twelve, less than I thought," Josiah says with a sense of relief.

Fifteen minutes later, Josiah see's Viola's face.

"Stop!" He examines the picture. "That's her, the girl I saw." Athena looks at Josiah.

"Are you sure?" Athena asks him. Josiah studies the girls headshots once more before confirming the girls identity.

"Positive."

"Fetch Atticus and Markus, we're going to London."

*

Athena, Josiah, and his brothers Atticus, and Markus, the eldest of the three brothers, find themselves standing in front of a town house in Dulwich Village. Athena rings the doorbell, moments later a man in his fifties, around five foot ten, stocky, with grey hair, opens the door, recognises Athena and smiles a warm, welcoming grin. She smiles.

"Hello, Alastair, we had an unexpected visit from Lola today."

"You had better come in then." Alastair holds the door open for them, they all walk past him, entering the house. Alastair shows them into the lounge. It was a homely house Josiah thought; as you entered through the front door, there were the stairs, taking you up to the first floor. The flooring that ran through the hallway was made from a dark wood, as were the stairs. The walls were painted a light shade of grey, the skirting boards and door frames had been painted white. The walls were lined with family photographs. The lounge walls were painted white; the fireplace, the mix of antique, and country home décor brought a cosy, warm, welcoming feel to the place. Alastair offers them all a drink, which they all politely declined.

They turn to face the lounge door, as they hear keys turning in the front door.

"Lola!" Alastair calls out as he hears Lola enter through the front door. As she begins to make her way up the stairs, to her bedroom, her dad, looking rather flustered, pokes his head out from behind the lounge door. "Lola, we have guests. They have come to see you."

With her face baffled, she follows her father into the lounge. As she enters, she recognises one of them instantaneously, the young man from the manor house, she also recognises the lady. Athena stands to shake Lola's hand; the three young men follow.

"Viola?" Athena says offering a hand out for Lola to shake, she takes Athena's hand and shakes it.

"Lola."

"My name is Athena, this is Josiah, you may recognise him from earlier?" Josiah raises an eyebrow, as she takes his hand, it felt warm and clammy against her own.

"From the manor house, you visited earlier...," he says dryly. Lola drops her hand and looks at her father, her father returns her anxious look with a calm smile.

"This is Atticus." As Lola takes Atticus's hand in hers, a warmth possesses her fingertips, which continues to spread throughout her fingers, and up her arm. "This is Markus." Lola shakes the third brother's hand. "Please sit down, we have a lot to talk about," Athena insists. Lola perches herself on the edge of a herringbone grey armchair. Alastair places himself on the arm next to her.

"Athena is an old friend of the family. They are here to help you," Alastair says reassuringly.

"Help me with what?" Lola replies. Alastair looks at Athena, and at the three young men, he places a comforting hand on Lola's shoulder.

"To inform you, why we are the way that we are, to explain." Lola looks at her father, Athena, Atticus, Josiah, and Markus. She could tell they were brothers, although they did not look entirely alike, they did resemble one another. The same eyes, the same medium—with tones of honey—brown hair, the same jaw line, and freckles. Josiah resembles Markus the most in the sharpness of his features, Atticus has striking features also, but they appear softer. All of them tall, and broad shouldered, they remind her of three friendly, handsome giants; but somehow, they had a look about them, like they do not belong in this time, but from a time hundreds of years ago. A time when boys and men wore stylish clothes, tailored waistcoats, and trousers, and were gentleman. She could imagine them as pilots, fighting for their country in one of the great wars that she had read about in history books.

"I remember you from the house," she says, studying Josiah. "I also remember you," studying Athena, "You have visited us before. I was ten. I was upstairs reading, and I heard an unfamiliar voice talking to my parents. I came and sat on the stairs, trying to listen. I could not hear the conversation, but I did see you, when you left."

"Yes, I remember. I had come to speak to your parents, about you, that is why your father knew to be expecting my return," Athena replies. The atmosphere quietens.

"So, tell me. Explain to me, why are we, the way that we are?" Lola says directly.

"Feisty, isn't she?" remarks Josiah, Atticus gives Josiah a stern look. The three friendly, handsome giants look at Athena, Athena continues.

"Thousands of years ago, some of the Greek gods visited Earth's plane and mated with mortals, with humans; this created a different kind of human species, called Nephilim. History, myths, and legends refer to them as Giants," Lola scoffs.

"Greek gods, Nephilim, giants, these are all stories."

"Well, stories have to originate from somewhere." Josiah's voice was sharp and possessed a tone of boredom. *Maybe I was wrong about the friendly assumption* Lola thinks, she narrows her eyes at Josiah, then turns her attention back to

Athena.

"Don't be rude, it is a lot to process," Atticus says interfering. Lola felt her heart lift. Josiah stops examining his fingernails and looks at Atticus. Although twins, Atticus and Josiah are opposites. Where Josiah is brash and imperious, Atticus is reserved and benevolent. Lola studies them both; well, maybe the friendly assumption was correct, just not for *all* of them. Lola suddenly feels herself appreciative towards Atticus.

"Continue," Lola instructs.

"The giants were not like the giants that have been written about in fairy tales. Thousands of years ago the average height for a male was between five foot three and five foot five. When Nephilim were born, they grew a foot taller, sometimes even a foot and half taller. The average Nephilim male height was between six foot three and seven foot, the females between five foot ten and six foot three. As evolution took place and the Nephilim mated with mortals, their height decreased. However, although physical appearances changed, those who continued to possess strands of the gods' DNA, still obtained some abilities. Extra strength, the ability of sight; to see, and dream of the past. Past lives I mean, and the future, the ability to heal. Some, of whom you may have heard of; Nostradamus, Noah, Jesus, Moses, Pythia, Edgar Cayce's, Leonardo DaVinci.

But over time, their abilities started to subdue. In the sixteenth Century, a group of scientists formed an underground group, calling themselves the 'Society of Genetic Engineering', the S.G.E. for short, specialising in the research of diseased human cells; the disease being the strand of the god's DNA. Not long after the big shift, many more Nephilim started to wake. The scientists surfaced, approaching the most powerful political leaders, showing them their research, that is when it became mandatory that with every new-born, a vial of their blood had to be taken.

Not long after, the scientists created a microchip that could replicate the DNA strand. They have not yet discovered where the strand originate from, but they are aware that people with the dormant strand of DNA, once activated, can possess certain abilities, but the chip can also deactivate a Nephilim. What they have not yet discovered, is that if a child has been born from two active Nephilim parents; in other words, a full-bloodied Nephilim they have the potential to also become a time-traveller. My father Zeus saw this danger in advance; the danger that when the governments discover the strand, start withdrawing the blood, and create the micro-chip, the impact it would have on both the mortal and Nephilim races; it was then my father, Zeus, sent myself, and my siblings back here to Earth plane. We were all placed in a vicinity near a dolmen. I was placed at Pentre Ifan, where you, Lola, came through. Dolmens are scattered world-wide, they are portals created by the gods to travel around the globe, and through time. Stonehenge is one of them, as is Pentre Ifan. Full-bloodied Nephilim, and the gods are the only ones who can use them. When we touch them, and think of a place, or a person we would like to go to, or see, when touched, it brings you out of the nearest Dolmen to them."

"That explains, why I ended up at the house, when I touched it. A warmth spread through me, then you popped into my head, I thought about when you had visited," Lola informs Athena.

"I am here, we are here, to ask you if you would like to

join us once you have completed your higher education of course. You were a child born to two active Nephilim; we can train you to control your abilities. My father Zeus has foreseen a great danger approaching, somebody is going to try and change Earth's history. We need individuals with the potential to become a traveller, to help us prevent them from accomplishing their aim. If we fail, the Sky Gods will attempt to extinguish the Earth plane once again. We cannot allow that to happen."

"Again?"

"I am sorry Lola, we are not allowed to tell you anything further until you agree to join us."

"Can I have time to think?" Lola asks. Athena stands, the three handsome giants follow suit.

"Of course. Alastair has my phone number. When you have made your decision, give me a call. We understand it is a decision that cannot be made on a whim, no judgment will be placed upon you, whatever you decide."

*

"Atticus! Atticus!" Atticus's eyes burst open; his night shirt wet through with sweat. He looks up to see Josiah's concerned face hovering above him.

"Was it one of your dreams?" Josiah asks him. Atticus shakes his head.

"No, this one was different, I was walking through a dark place, being followed by shadows."

"Have you told Athena about them yet?" Josiah asks with concernment. Atticus shakes his head.

"No, I don't want to bother her, she already has enough

on her plate." Josiah studies his brother's face, he notices beads of sweat on Atticus's temples, and dark circles under his eyes.

"Your dreams disquiet me. They could be a warning."

"They're just night terrors Josiah, no cause for concern. They are just anxiety dreams. Sorry for waking you." Atticus watches his twin walk back to his bed. Letting out a sigh, Atticus attempts to fall back to sleep. As he feels his eyes start to drift shut, an image of a swarm of bees chasing him, and the sound of a woman's scream enters his mind.

*

Warsaw, the year: 1939.

Celestyna pulls over in her Rolls Royce Wraith, along one of the dull grey streets of Warsaw. As she exits the car, closing the door behind her, she glances around, checking that nobody was around, she pulls out a pocket-knife from her purse and pierces one of the tyres. Moments later Stefan appears.

"Excuse me sir!" she calls out to him, Stefan stops, turning to face her.

"Madam."

Celestyna flashes him a smile.

"Would you mind helping me with my tyre."

Stefan looks down at the tyre and smiles.

"It would be my pleasure." Stefan follows Celestyna to the trunk of her car and lifts the lid.

"Er…" Celestyna looks down, the trunk is empty.

"Oh. Well, that could be a problem. How silly of me to forget to check the spare tyre holder." Celestyna laughs nervously, Stefan closes the lid.

"There is a repair store not far from here. I can show you."

"That would be lovely, thank you." Celestyna holds out her right hand, "Celestyna Zaborski." Stefan takes the tips of her fingers and shakes her hand.

"Stefan Zgrzembski."

"Not Stefan Zgrzembski, the lawyer?"

"The one and only."

"Oh, how funny! You are the man I was just on my way to see." Stefan starts to lead Celestyna down one of the sidewalks.

"You were?"

"Yes. My husband Filip was a client of yours, until he passed." Stefan stops to face Celestyna.

"I am sorry." Celestyna smiles, brushing Stefan's apology aside.

"It's the past." Stefan smiles, nods, and continues to walk. "He was a farmer. Before he passed, he wrote a letter signing over his land to me. He instructed me to hand deliver this letter to you personally." Celestyna stops, rummages through her bag, pulls out a letter and hands it over to Stefan. Stefan smiles, takes the letter from her, and begins to read it.

Dear Stefan,

Within this letter you will find my last will and testament. Upon my death I would like the deeds to my property to be placed in my wife Celestyna's name. The diagnosis of influenza apparently passed on to me via my dear hens, according to Dr Isrka, has prevented me from being able to travel to Warsaw myself to make the changes under your personal consult. I did try to call, but you were proven to be a difficult man to get hold of. My identity card, the copy of the deeds, and our marriage record are now in Celestyna's hands. Please help my beloved wife.

Your friend,
Filip Barnas

"You are Filip's wife? You do not look like how I imagined."

"What did you imagine?"

"Not any lady like yourself, someone older perhaps?"

"Someone nearer to his age?"

"I am sorry if I have offended you, Mrs Barnas."

"I am not offended, and please, call me Celestyna. My family were poor. Mr Barnas had lost his first wife, she was older, barren. He wanted a new wife, someone to provide him with an heir. I was young, and my family needed financial support. Although older, I did grow to love him Mr Zgrzembski. He was a good, kind man."

"He was indeed Mrs Barnas. This doctor, Dr Isrka, do you know how I may contact him?"

"Sadly, no. Not long after Filip's death, Dr Isrka also caught the virus and passed a few days later."

"I see, that is most inopportune, Mrs Barnas."

"Celestyna, please," she insists again, Stefan smiles.

"Celestyna. Would you please kindly follow me to my office?"

*

East Dulwich, the year: 2048

As Lola wakes, she can hear the rain tapping against her window, a typical autumn day in London. "Akira," she says whilst stifling a yawn, the white plastic dome that is sat on Lola's bedside table lights up. A woman's voice, heavily layered with an Eastern European accent comes out of it; "Morning, Lola. How may I help you this morning?"

25

"Search, chased in forest, dream meaning."

"Dreaming about being chased through a forest indicates communication problems with others, or a certain individual, often the person chasing you."

"Completely unhelpful. Thank you, Akira." The machine's lights turn off. Lola turns onto her side, pulls out a notebook from under her pillow, sits up, propping herself up on one of her pillows, she picks up a pen from her bedside table and begins to write.

5 October 2048

The dreams are becoming more vivid. I was in a forest dancing to some beautiful music, but I was not alone, I could feel somebody else there with me, I could not see them. I only heard a man's voice telling me to run, and somebody, or something began to chase us, and then a sharp agonising pain shot up my leg from my ankle, which led me to wake.

With a sigh Lola closes her notebook and slides it back under her pillow. Smelling the whiff of freshly brewed coffee, she pulls on her dressing gown and makes her way down into the kitchen, where Alastair is already sitting at the breakfast table with a mug of coffee; milk, two sugars, just the way he likes it, and a bowl of porridge, with some honey and a sliced banana. Alastair is a creature of habit; he always had been as far back as Lola can remember. Pouring herself a cup of coffee for herself and a bowl of cereal, she joins him.

"The abilities, the dreams they mentioned about the past, the future, did they mean our past, I mean our previous lives?" Lola asks Alastair. He peers at Lola over his daily newspaper.

"Are you still having peculiar dreams?" he asks her with concern.

Lola glances at her father, it was not anything new to his ears, ever since Lola turned thirteen, she had started to dream, peculiar, vivid dreams, dreams about people and places from the past. People, places in which there was no way she could have ever known about, and yet when she researched the names and places she had dreamt about, she discovered that they had indeed once existed.

"Yes, I think they are all connected, but recently there have been other presences present. I can feel them, I cannot see them, but I know they are there."

"It is possible, I suppose. There is so much about the subconscious mind that is yet to be discovered. Athena would likely know more. Have you given any thought as to whether or not you will join them?"

"Some. A lot. Like Atticus said, it is a lot to process."

Alastair senses there is more to Lola's indecisiveness, as Lola picks at her cereal.

"What is it?"

"I… I am just not sure they have the right person."

"Why do you think that?" Lola places down her spoon.

"I don't know, I guess it seems like a pretty important calling, a calling for somebody who is a good person."

"And you do not think you are a good person?"
Lola picks up her spoon again and continues to push her cereal around the bowl with her spoon, avoiding her father's eyes.

"I know there are better, more deserving people."

"What makes you think they are better, more deserving?"

"Because trouble does not follow them wherever they go, because they are smarter, or because it is their first instinct to put others before themselves. Unlike me, trouble follows me, and I am selfish."

"Every person walking on this Earth is selfish, Lola, and

27

that is the way it should be, except for some circumstances. People may accuse you of being selfish because you are not doing what they want, or what they think is right, but then does that not mean that they too are being selfish by expecting you to do something that pleases them, that makes them happy? Rather than encouraging you to make choices that will help you, or make you happy? Our main aims being here are to learn, grow, and most importantly to be happy, that is all. Everybody has dark in them, everybody has light, you are just as good and deserving as those whose appear to be smarter, kinder. Athena would not have reached out to you, if she did not honestly believe that you could achieve the full potential of your abilities, and possess the character traits, and skills that they need. However, what is important is what you want, not what you think you deserve, or can achieve. Do you want to help them?"

"Yes, I think I do, but…"

"No but, if that is what your heart wants, then do not allow your head to enter the equation. Lola, I want you to be happy. Your mum would want you to be happy. To have no regrets. To live your life to the fullest and the only way to do that is to follow your heart, regardless of what you think you deserve, or should do, or what you think society expects."

Lola smiles at her father, he was right, if her Mum were alive, she would be offering her the same advice. She can tell he misses her, although he never shows it. She can tell that he misses the companionship, and wishes somebody wonderful would enter his life, and sweep him off his feet. A good woman, with a good heart. A woman with as much passion for life as he has.

"Call Athena."

Chapter Two

Pentre Ifan, 2048

Lola, Markus, and Athena are sitting at a large oak dining table with various fruits, vegetables, meats, and breads spread across it. Markus's plate is piled the highest, beside each plate stands a goblet of red wine. Rain is pouring down outside, the splashing against the glass-stained windows fill Lola with a sense of contentment. The large oak door that separates the dining hall and the hallway, opens wide. All three look up as Atticus, and Josiah enter the room drenched from the rain. Lola feels her cheeks flush at the sight of their shirts plastered against their healthy, strong torsos. Athena sighs, picks up the bell that is sitting beside her, moments later the family's butler Berty enters the dining hall.

"Berty please fetch some towels for Atticus, and Josiah, it seems they both forgot their raincoats again." The brothers sit, grabbing a plate each and start to pile up various meats, vegetables, and breads onto them. Berty nods and exits the room. Markus carries on eating; Athena is staring at the two brothers.

"Atticus, Josiah, we have company, it is rude not to acknowledge them." Lola peers around the exceptionally large chicken that was hiding her from view. Josiah, and Atticus look up from their plates, a big, welcoming, happy smile spreads across Atticus's face.

"Viola, you have decided to join us, welcome!" Atticus says gleefully.

"Lola, not Viola. Hello Atticus, I have. Athena, Markus, and I were just discussing my training, it all sounds rather exhilarating!"

"Exhilarating!?" Josiah looks at Athena.

"Yes Josiah, exhilarating. We are happy that Lola has decided to join us. I have already informed Lola that you will be her physical training tutor."

"Athena, you never…"

"Josiah, you have developed your physical abilities far beyond Markus and Atticus. You are the one who will be able to help Lola the most in that department. It has already been decided, you will be her physical teacher, Markus her tutor in our history."

"And what about Atticus?"

"Atticus will continue his physical training alongside you. Atticus and I are currently working on a project."

Josiah hesitates.

"Athena… "

"Josiah, this is non-negotiable. I am the head of this institute; therefore, I politely ask you to trust me, respect that, and not question my decisions." Josiah nods.

"I am sorry Athena, I do respect you, I will do as you request." Lola could feel Josiah's eyes upon her, burning a hole straight through her. Suddenly, she feels all the hairs on her arms stand up. Athena continues.

"From now, Lola will be staying at the institute every weekend. During Atticus, and Josiah's physical training, Markus will be teaching her theory; after lunch Josiah will be teaching her physical. Her evenings will be devoted to her higher education studies, any questions?" Josiah and Atticus shake their heads.

*

Atticus and Lola are walking down one of the corridors. Lola thought all the corridors throughout the house looked the same, all the floors are made of pine floorboards, the walls are all painted russet, and old painted portraits hung upon them. Being an archaeology student, Lola could not help but feel fascinated walking through the old manor, studying the structure, the décor, the different textures.

"I hope Josiah has not made you feel unwelcome?" Lola looks up at Atticus, she could tell he genuinely felt embarrassed about Josiah's response to her agreeing to join them and residing at the manor during the weekends.

"I feel Josiah does not like change, or he finds it difficult to trust strangers, a newcomer entering the mix. I think he did not expect me to consider Athena's offer to join you."

Atticus and Lola come to a stop.

"This is you," Atticus says jollily.

Lola looks at the large oak door. Atticus swings her bag off of his shoulder, she forgot to close her bag; Atticus being stronger than he realises, swinging the bag of his shoulder led to the contents of her bag to spill out onto the floor, including her dream journal. As Atticus helps Lola pick up her belongings, he sees the notebook.

"You keep a dream journal?"

Lola shoves her books back into the bag, remembering to close her bag this time.

"Yes, my dreams are unusual. I like to write them down,

31

so then I can look back on them, maybe research them, if in the dream an unusual name, place, or incident appears." Atticus smiles at Lola.

"Well, Goodnight," Atticus says, smiling a warm, gentle smile.

"Thank you for showing me to my room." Lola smiles.

"You are welcome. See you tomorrow." Atticus turns and strolls off back down the corridor.

Lola enters her room. As she looks around, she can see the walls, and floor decor match the rest of the house. It is a plain room, but beautiful. The room has a big window that overlooks the house's gardens; in the distance she can see the dolmen that she accidentally came through. The windows are framed with gold curtains, all the furniture is made of mahogany. Against one of the walls is a four poster, mahogany bed, a gold curtain is attached to the top frame. Against the wall, opposite the foot of the bed, is a dressing table, next to the table a long mirror, and on the other side of the table a wardrobe. Under the window, stood a chest of drawers. Lola sits down on the bed. As she looks around the room, she feels a familiarity.

*

Entering the institute's library for the first time took Lola's breath away, never has she stepped into such a strikingly beautiful library.

"Lola!" the calling of her name by Markus brings her back from her thoughts.

"Sorry, it's beautiful," Lola says as she continues to glance around.

"It is, this is mine, Atticus and Josiah's favourite room in the whole of the manor. I think the books remind us of our parents, they loved books."

"Do you miss them?"

"Yes, I think Josiah misses them the most." Lola can tell that talking about his parents, made him feel uncomfortable. She decides not to push the topic of their family's history further. Lola takes a seat at the large oak table that was placed in the middle of the library.

"Athena feels it is important to learn about our history and lineage. She feels by understanding it, it helps us to understand who we are, I agree. So today I am going to teach you about which gods, belonged to which generation, and what their powers were... are."

"Question; shouldn't Athena be the one teaching me this, since she is one of them?"

"Athena has more important things to be dealing with."

"Right." Lola feels taken back from Markus's blunt comment.

"Not that you are not important Lola, you are. Athena senses that whatever it is that is going to try and change history; she feels it is going to happen soon. Her, and Atticus are looking for other potentials. Attempting to recruit others to join our side."

"Of course. I mean I know there are more urgent matters that need to be attended to." Markus smiles at Lola reassuringly,

"Shall we continue?"

Markus walks over to one of the shelves and pulls out a thick, blood red, leather bound book, and places it on the table in front of Lola, taking a seat next to her. The book looks incredibly old, however, surprisingly it is in excellent condition.

"This book holds information about all the gods and goddesses, and which generation they belonged too, their abilities, which gods and goddess went on to produce the first Nephilim."

"Is there a way we can discover which ones are our direct ancestor?"

"I'm afraid not, Atticus, Josiah, and myself have asked Athena the same question. They had many children. Athena thinks whatever abilities we develop could be an indicator, but many of the gods shared similar abilities; it's virtually impossible to decipher which ones we are descended from, from that." Markus opens the book, Lola opens her workbook, to take notes as Markus dictates.

"There were six generations, including mortal, and immortal generations. The first generation; the Upper Sky God, and the first Primordial God, was Chaos. The second generation; the Sky Gods, and the second generation of Primordial Gods, those born from Chaos, were Tartarus, Gaia, Eros Elder, Erebes, Nyx and Uranus. Tartarus was the precursor to the underworld; Gaia, the personification of Earth; Eros Elder was the personification of light and love; Erebes, the personification of the dark; Nyx, the personification of night, and Uranus the personification of heaven. Uranus became Gaia's husband, together they created the third generation, the Titans. Mnemosyne, Tethys, Theia, Phoebe, Rhea, Themis, Oceanus, Hyperion, Cronus, Coeus, Crius, and Lapetus. It was Cronus, and Rhea's union that created the fourth generation, the Olympians. The Olympians were Zeus, Hera, Poseidon, Hestia, Demeter, Hermes, Ares, Athena, Hephaestus, Apollo, Artemis, and Aphrodite. The

Olympians gave birth to the fifth generation; the Argonauts, and the sixth generation, the Muses.

"As your homework I am going to ask you to study which Argonauts and Muses came from which Olympian. The Olympians that came to Earth's plane; the ones who created our race, the ones we descend from are Zeus, Aphrodite, Apollo, Poseidon, Ares and Boreas. Zeus' abilities are controlling the weather, movement of the stars, day, night, and the effects of time. Aphrodite; Amokinesis, and reality warping. Apollo; solar, and light manipulation, healing, and prophecy. Poseidon: aquatic manipulation, earth manipulation, strength, speed, and the ability to shapeshift. Ares; Telumkinesis, Ergokinesis, Electrokinesis, spell casting, teleportation and themokinesis. Boreas: the bringer of winter, and he controls the North wind. However, there seems to be a debate whether Boreas had children. Some say he married Oreithyia the daughter of the King of Athens, King Erichthonius and had four children, two daughters, and two sons. Others say he did not."

"Athena did not come to Earth also?"

"No, Athena decided to stay in Mount Olympus."

"Did she have any children?"

"No. She wanted to have children of her own, but she never did. Athena does not like to talk about her past. However, Athena took us in when Josiah and Atticus were only eleven, and I was thirteen, she raised us as her own. We grew to see her as a mother figure." Lola sees a distance leak into Markus's eyes. He snaps back. "Tea break?"

*

35

"How's the tutoring going?" Atticus says as he enters the Kitchen. Lola and Markus turn to look at Atticus. The sight of him dripping with sweat from his and Josiah's morning practical class makes her blush.

"It's a lot of information, but it seems to be registering," Lola replies. Atticus opens the fridge door and takes out two bottles of water.

"Tea break already?" Josiah asks as he enters the kitchen to join Atticus on their break from their training.

Lola turns at hearing Josiah's voice; she feels her cheeks flush again. Atticus throws him one of the bottles, as he joins him leaning on one of the work tops.

"I had forgotten how mind-blowing it is at first, hearing about our heritage. I felt a tea break was necessary before I caused Lola's head to detonate."

"Although, that would have been an interesting sight, it sounds like you made a wise choice; it would have been such a waste otherwise, to see such a pretty head such as hers plastered all over the walls." Lola becomes aware of sudden butterflies fluttering around in the pit of her stomach upon hearing Josiah's compliment. Changing the subject, Atticus suggests that his and Josiah's break is over. The two brothers exit, and Lola feels a sudden confusion; Josiah had always been sharp, unwelcoming towards her, and now he is paying her backhanded compliments, she feels the feeling of antipathy towards him shift within her.

*

The practical room is not how Lola imagined it to be. First, it is not a room, it is what Lola thinks must have once been a barn. A concrete bridge with beautiful arches had been built to connect the two buildings, and as she and Josiah cross it, she notices the most spectacular view of the manor's gardens. When she first heard there was a room dedicated to Nephilim practical training, she imagined it to look like the rooms she had read about in fantasy books. Rooms filled with weaponry, cabinets and shelves filled with all different sized swords, grenades, archery equipment and other kinds of weapons. Instead, it is filled with sports equipment such as trampolines, floor mats, various balance bars, gymnastics horse's, high bars, and multiple cardio machines and weights.

"Not what you expected?" Josiah asks Lola. Lola looks over at Josiah.

"I expected there to be more weapons."

"First lesson of the day, the most lethal weapon, if trained correctly, is yourself. When Athena feels you are ready to receive your physical weapon, she will request Nephilim Rashida to come and assess you. You will receive your weapon once your assessment is complete. Rashida will take your results back to Olympia, there your weapon will be forged. Until then…" Josiah looks around the room at the equipment.

"Until then, I must train my body to become the weapon."

"Exactly! And not just that, as part of our practical training we also receive healing training from Panacea."

"Who is Panacea?"

"Panacea is Athena's great niece."

"What happens during the assessment?"

"You will be asked to find solutions to certain obstacles, tested to find your strongest attributes, and to determine what your abilities are, or what potential abilities you may develop. I suggest that you focus on the now, strengthen your mentality, your senses, and physical strength." Josiah eyes Lola up and down, studying her. "You look strong." Josiah goes to touch Lola. "May I?" Lola nods. Josiah examines Lola's posture. "Your back needs straightening. Your upper spine curves slightly at the top. Shoulders are slightly slouched forward." With the palm of one hand, Josiah adds some support to Lola's core, with the other he gently pushes her shoulders back. "Your core is weak. Stand on one leg." Lola does as he says, only losing balance slightly. "Balance isn't awful." Josiah walks around her, places his hands on her hips. With Josiah standing so close, she could feel tension between them occur. It was not an unpleasant feeling, just strange.

"Sturdy hips. No imbalance. Good. Okay."

"Okay?" Lola responds. Josiah finishes his examination of her.

"I think the best place for us to start, is to focus on strengthening your core. Strengthening your core will lead to improving your posture, which will lead to balance improvement." Josiah walks over to one the walls where some floor mats are resting. He carries two of them over to a space on the main floor, drops them, and rolls them out. Lola walks over to him.

"First we need to warm up." Josiah makes them both run laps around the hall, occasionally switching between butt kicks, high knees, knee touches, toe touches, and arm swings. He moves them over to the mats; there they continue with stationary stretches and body conditioning stretches. By the end of the warm-up, Lola feels exhausted, she cannot believe how unfit she is. Josiah has Lola working with a balance board, accompanied by his support for the next part of the lesson, she understands now why when she had seen Josiah and Atticus in the kitchen, they were as sweaty as they were. She had not been more aware of how repugnant she must currently be; she wishes somebody different had been assigned to her as her practical teacher. She cannot deny that like his brother Atticus, she also found Josiah handsome.

*

Athena and Atticus are in the computer room. Both of them are laying on hospital beds, the back of the beds are raised. Wires are protruding from behind their napes, connecting them to one another. If somebody were to walk in on them, it would be no surprise if they thought they had walked in on a scene from film 'The Matrix'.

"Atticus?" Atticus looks around. He is in the middle of some woods; he turns to face where Athena's voice had called to him from.

"Athena?"

In the space between two large fir trees, Athena appears wearing a white chiton dress, her honey blonde hair is wavy, and flows down to her waist. Atticus looks at himself, he is still him mentally, but looking down at himself, his skin is tawnier, the hair on his arms is darker, and he feels taller, and stronger. He looks at Athena. Athena smiles again.

"It is okay Atticus, it is perfectly normal that when participating in a past life regression, you take on the physical form of who you were in that lifetime."

Atticus feels the blast of the sun's heat beaming on his skin. He looks up at the sky, he has never seen such a beautiful sky; he looks down at Athena.

"Where are we?"

Athena continues to walk towards him, picking a flower as she approaches him, she looks around at the woods that surround them. Atticus had never seen Athena this at ease before, it suited her, it made her face appear softer, more open.

"We are in Greece, a long, long, long time ago." Atticus hears a giggle come from behind one of the trees, and quickly turns to face the direction it came from. Athena smiles,

"A tree nymph, they were quite common during this time." Athena conveys. "Let us walk."

"How is this going to help me with my dreams?"

"If you can understand where the dreams are rooted from, then you can control them. The dreams fill you with fear Atticus and a build-up of fear can lead to a Nephilim's instincts being blocked. Your instincts are what we rely on for our survival, one misjudgement could mean the death of us. Being in tune with our intuition is intrinsic."

Atticus hears the giggle again and looks back towards the trees.

"I think we are being followed." Athena smiles, looks over her shoulder towards the area where the giggle came from, and stops walking.

"You need to know that your dreams are a result of past life memories. Past life Atticus. Although we can travel through time, and that being a Nephilim from two Nephilim parents, means you are able to travel through time; Nephilim cannot travel to a time where they are currently incarnated in another body, which means, even if you wish to change something about a past life, you cannot. You need to keep reminding yourself that your dreams are memories, memories that cannot be changed and that every life is different. You create your life, what we believe, we create." Athena looks up at the sky. "I miss this feeling, the ancient Greek sun beaming

on my skin. It always filled me with much contentment."
Athena can see the cogs going around and around in Atticus's
brain, she can see his thoughts consolidate.

"If we can control our dreams, then can we control the
outcome of a dream?" he asks her.

"You cannot control the outcome of a dream; you can only
control your emotions during a dream. You can choose to take
certain actions, but no matter your actions, the outcome will
still be the same; because our subconscious is stronger than
our conscious whilst we are in dream state. Especially if the
dream is a past life memory. It cannot change because it has
already happened. Let me show you. We are currently in a past
life simulation? Yes?" Athena asks Atticus, Atticus nods,
Athena looks around, she picks a flower, simultaneously the
flower remains unpicked. Athena laughs at Atticus's
flummoxed face. "Look."

Athena points to a tree, the nymph comes out from behind
it. Atticus feels his breath catch as his heart jumps; she is the
most beautiful woman he had ever seen. Her ruby red hair is
tied up with green vines threading themselves through it; loose
stray strands frame her heart shaped face, and she is wearing a
long emerald green tunic. A vine is tied around her waist
enhancing the curves. A moment later he sees himself in his
past life coming up behind her, wrapping his arms around her.
He turns the nymph around, and they kiss passionately, and
fall to the ground. Atticus feels the passion and excitement fill
him. Athena looks at the nymph and past life him, then at
Atticus, his face has become flushed.

"Remember this is a memory. I think that is enough for
today," Athena says, ending the past life regression session,
pulling Atticus and her back to the present, back to the manor,
back to the manor's computer room.

*

The trampoline is higher than Lola thought it was going to be, the frame is level with the top of her ribcage. She looks at Josiah, who has a big cheeky grin on his face.

"Up you get," Josiah tells her. Lola places her palms onto the edge of the trampoline, and attempts to lift herself up onto it, after a few struggled attempts she asks for Josiah's assistance. He stands close behind her, feeling his breath in her hair, he places his hands on her hips, Lola's body fills with electricity. After a count to three Josiah lifts her up onto the trampoline, joining her seconds later. He takes her hands in his; his hands feel warm, and clammy in hers again, like the first time they shook hands.

"Have you ever been on a trampoline before?"

"At secondary school we had trampoline lessons, my friend bounced off and broke her arm," She replies. Lola looks again at how high from the floor the trampoline stands.

"I promise you; I will not allow you to bounce off." Josiah starts to gently jump up and down, Lola joins him, gaining a feel for the trampoline's springiness. After five minutes of jumping up and down, Josiah lets go of her hands, and tells her to jump up and tuck in her knees. On the third attempt Lola succeeds in fully tucking in her knees. They carry on practicing the tuck jump for a while, until Josiah tells Lola he feels she is ready for the next step and asks for her permission to hold the back of her top, and to place his other hand behind her thighs, which Lola agrees to. Josiah almost pulls Lola backwards when he wraps her top around his hand, which startles her. She had never felt more aware of someone else's body so close to hers, and how sweaty they both were.

"Sorry," Josiah says softly into her ear.

"It's okay." The training room door swings open full force, Atticus steps in, Josiah could not have stepped back from Lola quicker.

"There's been an S.G.E. alert," Atticus informs them both before pausing for a moment staring at Lola and Josiah and before exiting the room. Josiah releases Lola's shirt from his grip.

"Until next time." On that, he jumps down from the trampoline, leaving Lola stranded.

Chapter Three

Josiah catches up with Atticus in the corridor. Josiah feels that Atticus is currently having a 'wall up' moment, and sighs. He wishes his brother would take more risks, open up more. Although he has always been physically affectionate towards people, as soon as he meets somebody who could really mean something to him, somebody he could see himself developing more than a plutonic friendship for, he puts up an emotional wall. He could tell that Atticus was developing a feeling of protectiveness towards Lola, a key indicator that she is someone Atticus could see himself developing intimate romantic feelings for. The emotional 'wall up' was something that has always been an Atticus thing. He often thought about what the cause of this could be, maybe it had something to do with what happened to them when they were children. Josiah looks at his brother and furrows his brows.

They meet Athena and Markus in the computer room. Markus is in their olive-green uniform which they wear out on the field. The material they are made from, was designed by Rashida herself, they are made with some kind of Nano technology. When the uniform gets ripped, or torn, it repairs itself, they were made to be resilient against most weapons. As Atticus and Josiah approach them, Markus throws them their uniforms, and they start to change whilst Athena briefs them of the mansion.

"Some S.G.E. soldiers have attempted to take a Nephilim, boy. The boy luckily escaped and was able to find a safe place to hide. It will not be long before they discover where he is by the chip's tracking device; maybe 20 minutes."

"He's chipped?" Josiah shakes his head at the thought of Nephilim parents wanting to chip their child, like some pet dog, or cat. Athena turns to face them.

"I am sending you the location now." The little screen on their leather wrist communicator bands flash. Josiah and Atticus head towards the door, Markus shouts,

"Where are you going? I can teleport us there!"

"Teleport?" Atticus laughs. He and Josiah walk back towards their brother, they notice that his uniform had new hoops attached to it on the upper arms, where other people can hold onto him as he teleports; teleporting not only Markus, but the passengers that are holding onto him too.

"Hang on!" Markus instructs. Josiah and Atticus each take hold of a hoop. They feel themselves being sucked into thin air, then a popping sound, as they feel their feet land firmly on some hard, solid ground.

"I think I'm going to throw up." Atticus and Markus look at Josiah and laugh.

The brothers look around. They had landed in a dark, damp cave. Markus's communicator beeps, he presses one of the buttons a map projects from it. On the map are three little green dots that represent them, a little yellow dot, the Nephilim boy in trouble. Not far from them, outside of the cave, five dark grey dots were also showing, heading in their direction; the S.G.E. soldiers.

"Five against three, easy." Josiah says. They start to head towards the little yellow dot, which led to the boy. He was crouched behind a boulder. The boy looks to be the age of around thirteen. The boy notices that the brothers are wearing the green uniform of the Nephilim guard. Atticus kneels next to him, placing his finger on his own lips, instructing the boy to remain quiet. Then gently stands back up. The three brothers walk back towards where they teleported in, a golden bow and arrow appear on Atticus's back, some golden knuckle dusters appear on Josiah's hands, and a sword and shield appear in Markus's hands. They hide above the cave's entrance. When the first three S.G.E. soldiers enter the cave, the brothers leap onto them, taking the soldiers by surprise. The two free S.G.E. soldiers following behind pull out their swords, and charge to assist their fellow soldiers in trouble.

Atticus and Josiah tackle down their soldiers. Josiah punches his victim, freezing him in place. Atticus pulls out one of his golden arrows and stabs his next victim in the shoulder sending him into unconsciousness. They look at their brother, who has the other three S.G.E soldiers fighting him. Josiah punches the ground sending ripples towards them, causing two of the soldiers to lose their balance. Atticus shoots two of his arrows towards them, which hit them both just below their hearts. Before one of his arrows had hit their targets, one of them had thrown a dagger at Josiah, hitting him in his side knocking the wind out of him and injuring him. Josiah falls back against the cave wall, the force of his body crashing against the cave walls causes one of the boulders to fall onto him, trapping him, pinning him to the cave floor. Although wounded and trapped, Atticus can see that Josiah is okay and carries on assisting Markus. Atticus pulls out another arrow and shoots the last attacker, but not before the last S.G.E. soldier cuts Markus's side with a dagger he pulls out of his right boot. Markus stumbles over to help Atticus with the fallen rock, although weakened, together they lift the rock off Josiah.

"The boy," Josiah says under his breath. Whilst Markus remains with Josiah, Atticus goes to check on the boy who was still hiding behind the boulder, unharmed, but clearly in shock.

"It's okay, you can come out now. They can no longer harm you," Atticus says to the boy. The boy and Atticus make their way back to Josiah. The boy looks over at the frozen, unconscious soldiers.

"They cannot be taken out of their unconscious states until the Nephilim who put them in it, removes the magic; the magic from the arrow that shot them." Atticus ruffles the boys hair and smiles. The boy looks between Markus and Josiah.

"Will he be okay?" the Nephilim boy asks. Josiah laughs.

"It's just a flesh wound, and my ribs are a bit bruised, but I'll live."

Atticus and Markus help their brother up. Markus informs the boy that they will take him back to their institute, where his parents are waiting for him.

The first trip back to the institute from the cave, Markus takes the boy and Josiah. When they arrive back at the manor, the boy's parents embrace him, Athena rushes to support the wounded Josiah. Markus teleports back to the cave to collect Atticus, but as he lands, he collapses.

"Markus!" Atticus catches him before he lands on the floor, he looks down at his brother's side where the S.G.E. soldier had cut him. Markus's clothing is soaked through with blood. Atticus lifts his brother's top to look at the wound, he see that he has been poisoned, and the poison has entered his blood stream. The area surrounding the wound was slowly

47

turning black. It looks like a tree with bare branches, and the bare branches were growing, spreading their long, thin fingers bit by bit. Markus can see Atticus is trying to think fast, he glances down towards the cut, then back up to Atticus's face.

"What is it?" Markus asks anxiously. Atticus looks between his brother's wound and his paling face.

"You have been poisoned. The blade must have been coated."

Markus puts his head back, resting it on the cave wall behind him.

"It's okay, Panacea is at the manor. I can call Athena and she will send Panacea to us and then she will be able to teleport us back to the institute and treat the poison." Markus looks at his brother, and smiles. Atticus presses some buttons on his communicator band, it projects an image of Athena's face.

"Atticus?"

"Markus has been poisoned. We need Panacea." Atticus informs her. Athena shouts something over her shoulder, moments later Panacea's face appears on the projection, next to Athena, peering over Athena's shoulder.

"Atticus listen to me; you are a spell caster." Panacea informs him.

"I'm a what?"

"A spell caster. Don't think, just listen to me. I need you to place your hands over the wound and keep repeating these words until I am able to reach you. 'Aporripste to dilitirio'."

Atticus does what she says and starts to repeat the words with her, "aporripste to dilitirio, aporripste to dilitirio."

"Good, Atticus. It will help subdue the poison, until I get there."

"Hurry!" Atticus says to her, Panacea's face disappears

from sight. Athena cuts off the call. Markus's face is starting to regain some colour. Atticus looks down at the wound, the poison that had started to spread has slowed down to an almost stop, he smiles.

"I think it's helping." Atticus reassures Markus.

His hands feel like they are burning, he keeps repeating the words Panacea told him to say. Atticus looks at his hands he sees a beautiful golden glow flaming from them. Markus looks up at his brother.

"A spell caster, eh?" Markus says with a faint chuckle. Atticus shrugs his shoulders.

"Both Mum and Dad were spellcasters, maybe she was hoping I had inherited it." Atticus continues to repeat the words. Markus looks down at his wound.

"Well, I'm happy she did."

They hear a popping sound next to them as Panacea arrives, carrying some leaves. She kneels next to them and asks Atticus to continue holding his hands above the wound and to keep repeating the words. "They're Capparis Tomentosa leaves, they help draw out poison."

As Panacea applies the leaves to the wound, Markus lets out a sigh of relief. She places her hands on the brothers, and they are all sucked back to the manor.

*

Lola knocks on Josiah's bedroom door. He calls to her to enter; he is sitting up in his bed wearing an old grey tee, reading a book. She walks over to his bedside, before she reaches it, Josiah has taken off his T-shirt revealing the bandage covering the shallow wound just under his chest. It had become routine over the last two days; as part of her first aid training she would clean and re-dress Josiah's wound twice a day. They sit in silence, she feels Josiah's eyes watching her with intense observation. She lets out a sigh.

"How are you feeling?" she asks him.

"It's healing speedily." Josiah replies. *Silence.*

"Athena has instructed that I am to carry on with my physical training, with Atticus as my teacher." Lola glances up at Josiah, to see if the updated information has led to a reaction, his face is unreadable.

"Atticus is a good teacher. Do you have a date for your assessment yet?" Josiah asks her.

"Not yet." Lola glances up at Josiah, he's flinching as she cleans his wound.

"What happens during the assessment?" she asks him curiously.

"Athena hasn't told me much about how they assess us." Josiah answers her curiosity.

"There are three stages within the assessment. Mental, physical, and to assess your abilities, which will also include assessing your reflexes. Have you seen the Nephilim map?" Josiah asks her. Lola nods, Josiah continues.

"Once you pass your assessment, and have received your weapon, you will become a little green dot, like us." A large, excited smile spreads across his face, like a child opening a present, revealing something they have been wanting for a very long time.

Atticus enters the room just as Lola is finishing applying the new dressing. Lola smiles at Josiah, "All done." Lola stands up.

"I'll come and change the dressing once more before

bed." Atticus smiles at her as she approaches the door to leave the room, he opens it for her to exit.

Atticus walks over to Josiah, "I thought I would check on you before my lesson with Lola."

"Yes, Lola did mention something about Athena requesting you to carry on preparing her for her physical assessment." Atticus seats himself on the edge of the bed next to his brother.

"Where has Lola reached in her training?" Atticus asks.

"We have covered no-handed cartwheels and somersaults, some weight training focusing on core strengthening, posture straightening, and flexibility. We had just started flicks, we got to flipping with assistance on the trampoline. She's a fast learner, a natural Nephilim warrior." Josiah informs him.

"And how are you doing brother?" Atticus asks.

"I am healing fast. I would think I should be fit enough within a week to continue Lola's training. I have seen you have started to grow fond of her?"

"You know me, I am a people person. I develop fondness for people within moments of meeting them." Atticus answers smiling. Josiah returns his brother's warm smile.

"You have always been the friendliest twin." Josiah comments. Atticus stands, before exiting the room Atticus turns and says over his shoulder to Josiah,

"You could be friendly too if you really wanted to be," Josiah chuckles. "Where would the fun in that be?" Atticus smiles and exits the room to meet Lola for their first lesson.

*

Lola is already seated on the trampoline in her training gear when Atticus enters the room carrying a notepad. In one swift movement he is on the trampoline with her, offering out his hand to help her up from her seated position

"Josiah informed me that you were amidst assisted flicks, so shall we start there?" Atticus asks her.

"Actually, we were just about to start when you were called to save the boy from the S.G.E."

Atticus places himself facing Lola's side. "May I?" Lola nods.

"You warmed up whilst waiting for me to arrive?" Lola nods again, Atticus wraps the back of Lola's top around his hand. She feels his fingers graze against her skin; and feels the warm tingle that she had felt, the first time he shook her head, it shoots up her spine. She felt Atticus freeze; he glances his eyes down towards her. As she looks up at him, he feels his breath catch, and smiles down at her. He places his other hand behind her thighs; the butterflies within her stomach start to flutter.

"On three you are going to jump into a tuck, you will feel pressure behind your thighs as I turn you over, but don't worry." Atticus tugs on her top. "I've got you. Just try to feel the movement of the flipping backwards. Ready?" Lola nods.

"One, two, three!" Lola jumps and tucks her knees in towards her chest. Atticus is strong, immensely strong. She is not a delicate girl, but when he turned her, she felt as if she were light as a feather.

"Good! That was good Lola." Lola looks at her hands, which are trembling, Atticus looks at her quivering hands.

"It's the adrenaline from the flip," he reassures her. Lola smiles, she knew the adrenaline wasn't the only reason why her hands were trembling. Atticus returns the smile. "Ready to do another?" he asks her. Lola nods.

"You will still hold on?" Lola asks him anxiously. Atticus tightens his grip on her top and takes a step closer to her.

"Of course. I will not let go of you until you say so, until you are ready." A voice inside her head softly speaks, *'You could hold onto me forever if you'd like,'* she feels blood pour into her cheeks. She cannot believe herself, her body. Her eighteenth birthday was approaching, and never in her eighteen years had a boy ever made her blush. She feels embarrassed by her bodies reaction to his touch, his voice, she is sure Atticus could see it; *'Maybe he will put the flustered redness of my face down to the exercise'*. She focuses on a spot on the wall opposite them.

"Okay?" Atticus asks her again. Lola nods.

"One, two, three." Atticus flicks her over, and she loses her balance again, Lola lets out a 'grr' sound of anger out in her frustration.

"Lola," Atticus says calmly, she looks at Atticus's hands which are currently placed on her hips

"There is still a minimum of a month before your assessment, you have plenty of time to master this, go easy on yourself, okay?" Atticus says, reassuring her.

"How do you know that?" Lola asks, looking up at him.

"Know what?" Atticus responds.

"That I still have at least a month to go before my assessment?" she replies ominously.

"Because we're not assessed until we have turned eighteen. It is your eighteenth birthday in the middle of next month, is it not?" Atticus asks her. Lola does not question him how he knows when her birthday is, instead she just nods, at which he smiles that heart wrenching smile of his and insists they carry on.

*

Lola enters the dining room. Athena had insisted on holding Lola a birthday party, and since her birthday was two days before the mortal holiday Valentine's Day, she had decided that the theme should be Valentine's, looking around, Athena had conjured up the corniest Valentine's decorations, Lola had ever seen.

"A glass of champagne for the birthday lady?" Markus plants a traditional champagne flute in front of her face, Lola takes the glass from him, noticing that he was on the soft drinks, he must still be healing from the poison. Lola looks around at the guests, and notices that Atticus is surrounded by four or five girls, as is Josiah.

"I do not know who any of these people are," Lola says under her breath to Markus. Markus looks at the girls surrounding his younger brothers.

"The girl with the ginger hair is Teresa." Markus points towards her and continues on to the other girls surrounding Atticus. "Then you have, Brigita, Helena, and Annie." Lola cannot help but notice how much flirting is happening between Atticus and Brigita. They are all over each other. She feels her gut go topsy turvy; *am I jealous?* Lola has never experienced jealousy before, she doesn't like it.

"Does Atticus like Brigita?" Lola asks Markus. Markus laughs.

"No, well at least I do not think he does. They have known each other for years. She may be interested in him, in fact I am sure of it, but I think he just sees her as a little sister," Markus

54

informs her. Lola studies Brigita, she cannot deny that Brigita is extremely attractive and is sure she can likely have any man she chooses. She continues to watch them; Atticus places his arm around Brigita's shoulders, and places a kiss on the top of her head. Something she has noticed about Atticus, is that he is an overly affectionate man, he hugs and kisses everyone, everyone except her. He did for the first month or so of them meeting each other, but then he just stopped. Looking at how open he is currently being with Brigita, and the other girls, agitated her. She instead turns her attention towards Josiah.

"And what about Josiah? Who are they?" Lola continues to enquire. Markus looks over to Josiah and points to each girl as he names them.

"Clara, Marie, and Sasha."

"And does Josiah like any of them?"

"Not any more. He and Marie were together a few years ago, but apart from that, no, not anymore." Lola continues to study Josiah, although physically affectionate, it is nothing compared to Atticus. *'Maybe my affections are falling for the wrong brother?'*

"And what about you?" Lola asks Markus, he chuckles.

"What's so funny? You are a handsome man, Markus, smart, and kind. Surely you must have women throwing themselves at you too?" Markus has a sip of his drink and looks down at Lola.

"A few, no more than the usual male Nephilim." He replies.

"What do you mean?" she responds, puzzled.

"Look around," Markus instructs. Lola looks around the room, there were only about ten males, the rest were females. She looks up at Markus. Markus continues "We are a dying breed, well the full Nephilim blood males anyway," Markus informs her.

"That cannot be true?" Lola looks around at the room again. "I don't understand. Why?"

"The S.G.E. When Nephilim parents started to side with the S.G.E. in the belief that Nephilim warriors should be chosen. The majority of Nephilim males were, and continue to be deactivated by the S.G.E. When a Nephilim is deactivated, they are also disabled from their abilities; their abilities are taken from them, so when they have a child, unless the child has a mother, that is of Nephilim blood also, then the child is born completely mortal. Naturally, those Nephilim parents who have chosen not to side with the S.G.E. and have daughters, they want their daughters to partner with a fellow Nephilim, and well a male Nephilim born from two Nephilim parents, it's like hitting the jackpot." Lola glances around the room then back towards the women surrounding Atticus and Josiah.

"So, these women, they're only interested in your blood?" she comments with alarm.

"Gosh, you make it sound so morbid! But likely yes, although the Hardy brothers are a bunch of rather dashing gents, I am sure that is also why." Markus winks at Lola and laughs, a warm laugh once more before kissing Lola on one of her cheeks, wishing her a happy birthday and departing himself from her presence, making his way over to a pleasant looking brunette lady. Lola looks over at Atticus again, this time Brigita is spread across his lap, she feels annoyance starting to creep in.

"Hello." Lola is startled out of her moping. In front of her, stood a man with jet black hair, and a handsome face; '*Are all*

Nephilim males handsome?' She thinks, looking up at the strikingly beautiful man that stands before her.

"Hello," the man says again to her. The man's voice is lower than any of the brothers', but just as smooth and friendly. He holds out his hand, Lola allows him to shake her fingers.

"Henri, Henri, Hardy," he says, introducing himself. *'Hardy?'* He must be a relative of the brothers.

"You must be Lola?" Henri asks, sounding genuinely interested in her.

"I am," Lola confirms, answering his question. He takes a place beside her.

"Are you enjoying yourself?" Henri enquires, again sounding genuinely interested in her and whether or not she is enjoying herself.

Glancing between Josiah and Atticus again. "I'm not really into parties."

"Is that a no?" he asks with a tone of concern. Lola shakes her head.

"Athena and the brothers seem to be enjoying themselves, so I am happy." Lola snatches another glass of champagne from one of the loaded trays being carried past them by one of the catering staff. She feels Henri's eyes engrossed on her face.

"Well, you should be, a beautiful young lady like yourself. It would be devastating if you were not, especially being the birthday girl."

Lola bursts out laughing, spitting champagne all over herself and him. "Sorry! But where do your family come from? A beautiful young lady like yourself, it would be devastating!" She repeats back to him impersonating a terrible 'posh' accent.

Henri gently laughs, they laugh together. Atticus approaches them both.

"Henri, I have seen you have met our Lola." Atticus goes to put his hand on Lola's lower back, but she steps aside, leaving him to awkwardly place his hand into one of his trouser pockets instead.

"Excuse me, I think I need to get some air," Lola says, dismissing herself from the Hardy men's presence. Atticus, and Henri nod. Lola exits, making her way through the French doors that lead out into the manor's gardens.

Sitting on a stone bench in the gardens, Lola looks up at the sky. The night sky always calmed her. She starts to feel as if she is spinning slightly, she closes her eyes and takes some deep breaths.

"Lola, are you okay?" Atticus asks her softly. *Oh god, I do not want to see him, not right now*, she continues to keep her eyes closed, she feels him sit beside her.

"Have I done something to upset you?"

Lola takes another deep breath before opening her eyes to look at Atticus.

"No," Lola responds bluntly. There is an awkward silence between them, Lola looks back up at the sky.

"I saw you talking to Henri."

"Yes, he seems lovely."

"You look cold, maybe we should go back inside?" Atticus suggests. Lola looks at Atticus.

"I don't want to," her voice comes out sharp, with a tone of annoyance. She feel Atticus's energy change. He's annoyed.

"You know Henri…"

Lola looks at him, he is not annoyed, more agitated. "It doesn't matter. I am going to head back in." He stands for a moment just looking at her.

"Okay. I will see you later," she says, then turns back to

looking at the night sky. She hears him storm off in a huff back towards the party.

*

Lola is sitting on her bed, writing in her diary when she hears a knock on her bedroom door.

"Come in!" she instructs. Atticus enters her room, she closes her diary, he is drunk.

"It's just Henri, he's always been the favourite in our family." Atticus blurts out catching Lola off guard. Lola stands, walks towards him, and shuts the bedroom door. She places a hand on his arm to steady him as he continues his slurred speech, his breath wreaks of alcohol.

"He and his girlfriend, the perfect couple. Everyone loves Henri. Everyone loves Josiah, everyone always likes Josiah; Josiah has always been considered the cute one. When I saw you talking with Henri and laughing? Everyone always likes Henri, Henri or Josiah," he continues to slur his words. "It's just-" Lola interrupts him before Atticus can continue with his drunken rambling, which she knows they will both regret later.

"I do not like Henri, or Josiah. You are the one I like, it's you I feel drawn to." Lola looks down embarrassed, '*Did I really just say that? Out loud?*' She looks back at Atticus who looks down and smiles, and then starts to open the door.

"Okay," he simply says, And on that, Atticus exits Lola's bedroom.

Chapter Four

Josiah and Atticus are standing outside the training room, waiting to wish Lola good luck before her assessments. As she approaches them, they both embrace her; Josiah giving her a big, tight, squeeze, which seems to have lasted longer than what is deemed appropriate. Atticus too gives her a tight hug, and the strangest thing happens immediately after, a feeling of a cartwheel firework happens within her chest, and she feels a huge power surge throughout her body. She suddenly feels highly energised, she imagines it was what the bunny in the old battery commercial, she once saw, would have felt like.

As she enters the room, a lady with skin, the colour of mocha is wearing a Nephilim guard uniform. Although her uniform is gold instead of the traditional olive green. The woman is Rashida; her hair is tied back into a ponytail; she is holding a computer tablet. When she sees Lola enter, she gives her a warm, friendly smile, and holds out her hand for Lola to shake, which eases Lola's nerves immensely.

"Hi, I'm Rashida." Lola takes Rashida's hand and shakes it. The trampolines and the other sporting equipment have been folded up, and are resting against the side walls, the other sporting equipment is packed away.

"Lola, has anyone told you anything about what we will be doing?" Rashida asks. Lola shakes her head.

"Josiah, a little," Lola answers. Rashida smiles.

"Well first I will say it's perfectly normal to feel nervous, but there is nothing to be fearful about." Rashida ties a watch around Lola's wrist, "So we can keep track of your pulse rate. I am just going to see what abilities you have; we can also tell what other abilities you may develop, that shall be the last assessment. The first assessment will be your physical fitness assessment. The second assessment will be mental, to see how you react under pressure, and how your brain works. The second and third assessments take place in a virtual setting." Rashida holds up what looks like a metal headband with a leather strap attached to it. "We place this over your eyes, and then the strap ties around the back of your head. What you see, I see on this." Rashida holds up the computer tablet to show Lola. "I will program in various tests. Once it is switched on, you will appear in a room with blank walls, which will change during each assessment. Follow?"

"Yes, I think so," Lola replies. Rashida smiles again.

"Good, if at any point you feel the need to pause, just say 'hold'. We do not mind if you wish to take a breather, we understand sometimes the assessments can feel intense. But for now, we will start on your physical."

Rashida walks over to an exercise mat which has been pre-set in the middle of the floor and asks Lola to stand on the 'X', which has been placed in the middle of the mat with some luminous yellow gaffer tape which stands out against the black surface of the mat. Rashida firstly asks Lola to do a simple double handed cartwheel, secondly a single-handed cartwheel, and then a no handed cartwheel. On the no handed cartwheel, Lola wobbles slightly on her landing but is able to keep her balance. Next Rashida requests her to do a variety of somersaults and backflips; again, on a couple of landings, Lola feels herself wobble but continues to plant her feet firmly onto the mat. After a quick water break, Rashida places the virtual reality band around Lola's eyes. As Lola looks around, she is standing in the middle of a white room, shaped like a cube, the walls are completely blank. The walls around her start to glimmer. On the wall, in front of her, appears a timer starting at two minutes; on the wall, next to the timer, appears a circle with a vertical line going through it. Next appears some random letters around the circle, above the circle the word Nephilim Guard appears; looking at the letters around the circle, they are all the letters needed to spell 'Nephilim Guard'. Lola knows exactly what she has to do. Using the letters around the circle she has to create the words 'Nephilim Guard' on the line, by moving them around in the circle before the clock runs out. This is the first exercise to see how she works under pressure. Rashida speaks.

"Lola?"

"Yes."

"Can you see the letters in front of you and the timer?"

"Yes."

"Do you know what you must do?"

"Create the words 'Nephilim Guard' along the line, using the letters around the circle before the timer runs out."

"Good. Ready?" Rashida asks her, Lola nods. The timer beeps, and Lola starts to push the letters back and forth around the circle, and as each letter is correct, she either slides it down, or up the line. So far, she has the letters Nephili and looks at the timer which is now showing only fifty seconds to go; Lola starts to speed up, she begins to feel failure creeping in and starts to panic. 'Breathe Lola,' she says to herself, and takes some deep breaths. She feels herself start to calm, with forty seconds left on the clock, she sees what she has to do; moving the letters around as fast as she can, one second left on the clock, she slips the 'D' into place, and shouts,

"Yes!" And laughs with relief. *I did it! I did it!* She knows her face is currently consumed with the biggest grin. Next to appear on the wall is a number problem, projected are the words, "Use all numbers, only using each number once. Symbols can be used a maximum of three times." On the wall she sees numbers 9,8,7,6,5,4,3,2,1 below is the number 100 with a question mark next to it. Next to the numbers appears a timer with a one-minute time limit.

"Lola, do you understand?"

"Yes, using the numbers I have to achieve the result of 100?"

"Correct. Ready?" Lola nods. *I can do this*, Lola reassures herself. Using her fingers, she starts to do her workings out, starting with seventy-six plus nine, plus eight, plus five, she erases the equation and starts again with ninety-eight minus six, plus five, minus three, minus one.

"No, two." She erases the writing and re-starts with ninety-eight minus seven, plus five, plus six, plus three, minus four. Lola lets out noise of annoyance and erases the working out. Ten seconds left; ninety-eight plus seven, plus six, minus five, minus four. Lola stops writing as the timer runs out, the feeling of defeat fills her. She hears Rashida's voice reassuring her.

"It's okay, Lola, it's a common occurrence the timer running out before the Nephilim has completed the task. Do not worry. I am now going to switch the programming to ability testing mode. Ready?"

Lola is not sure what to expect. In front of her appears a

S.G.E. soldier, and then tall oak trees appear surrounding her. Although Lola knows the S.G.E soldier isn't real, he certainly looks real. The soldier is holding up a sword, running towards her. Lola only knew one of her physical abilities; the ability to control anything linked to the earth, including tree roots, and vines. She discovered this recently whilst out exploring the countryside that surrounds the manor. She tripped over a tree root, and as she put her hands out instinctively to prevent herself from falling, she instead called out to some vines, to reach out to her, wrap around her waist, and pull her backwards, stopping her from falling flat on her face. Lola had been practicing doing this mentally ever since. Using her mind, she calls upon roots that are buried beneath the foundation of the old barn to wrap around the soldier's sword and pull it from his grip, wrap themselves around his legs. A knife appears in the soldier's hand, he cuts the roots from around his legs, freeing them, and continues to run towards her. Lola hides behind one of the trees, she feels adrenalin pumping through her veins. A wave of warmth sweeps over her; feeling like heat from the sun on a 40 degree Celsius day. Next, she finds herself surrounded by fire, she looks around for the soldier, but he has vanished. Looking at the fire, she raises her hands to protect her face from the heat of the fire, out of them sprays water, extinguishing the fire, taking Lola by surprise. The white walls that surround her vanish. Rashida is standing behind her untying the virtual band. As Lola looks around the room panting, she sees shreds of no the tree roots, and puddles of water scattered all over the floor.

"How did I do?" Lola asks still panting.

"Very well. Aquatic and Earth Manipulation, and you are a shapeshifter. I haven't come across one of those in a while…

not since your mother."

"A shapeshifter?" Lola knew of her Earth manipulation, but not of her shapeshifter or aqua manipulation ability.

"Yes. A shapeshifter, when you hid, you also became part of the tree." Rashida can tell by Lola's surprised face that she was not aware of what she had done.

"Did you feel a sudden wave of warmth sweep over you?" Rashida asks.

"Yes."

"That was when you changed. It is your weakest ability, but I shall inform Athena, she will be able to schedule some private shapeshifting lessons, to help strengthen it. I would advise that you tell no one of this ability. Shapeshifters are extremely rare, highly sort after. When a Nephilim shapeshifts into something, or someone, they also take on their powers so, as well as your own abilities remaining intact, you also possess the abilities of the person you have shapeshifted into. I think your mother was in fact the last Nephilim I knew that possessed the ability, bless her soul. You should receive your weapon by the end of the week. It was lovely to meet you Lola." Rashida shakes Lola's hand.

Lola exits the training room to find Atticus and Josiah are still there, waiting for her, sitting on the floor with their backs against the wall.

When she exits, they stand up, Josiah is the first to speak.

"How did it go? Did you pass?"

Lola grins with excitement.

"I did!" Lola says grinning. Josiah throws his arms around her, embracing her in a celebration hug. Atticus gives her a little hug and kisses her on the cheek.

"We knew you would." Josiah claps his hands together.

"We need to go and get your uniform, and the guard training gear." Josiah says excitedly. Lola looks at Josiah.

"There's a place to get them. I thought someone made them for you." Lola comments. Atticus smiles.

"Someone does, but first you need to get measured. Also, you need to inform the tailor of your abilities, because they make our gear to adjust to them." Lola stops in her tracks.

"Inform them of our abilities?" *'Rashida said I can't tell anyone that I'm a shapeshifter.'*

"Are you okay?" Atticus was looking at her with brows furrowed.

"Yes, fine." she mutters and fakes a reassuring smile.

"Atticus, of course Lola is fine, she has just become a fully pledged Nephilim warrior. Why wouldn't she be fine? Lola we must go tomorrow, straight after breakfast. Atticus, and I would be more than happy to take you. Wouldn't we?" Josiah looks at his brother waiting for his reply.

"Unfortunately, I will not be able to tag along this time. Athena and I are working on our project straight after breakfast tomorrow," Atticus responds. Lola is not sure if she imagined it, but when Atticus said he would not be able to join her and Josiah, she could have sworn she saw a little smile creep onto the sides of Josiah's lips.

*

Athena is sitting at her desk when Lola knocks. Lola had tried to catch her before breakfast, but she was busy, so thought this would be her last chance to speak to her before Josiah took her gear shopping. As Lola enters, she closes the door behind her, Athena see's she is anxious.

66

"Lola, is everything all right? Please sit down." Lola seats herself on the chair, opposite to Athena.

"Athena, I'm worried about my gear fitting. Rashida told me that I wasn't allowed to tell anyone of my shapeshifting ability, except you. Atticus mentioned to me that we have to inform the tailor of our abilities, because our gear is made to adjust to our abilities. I'm not sure what I'm supposed to do."

"It's all sorted. Josiah made me aware of your plans to sort out your gear today, I have contacted Aphrodite to assist you. She is placed near the tailor and will make out that she has to cover the Nephilim who originally would have done it."

"But won't Josiah think that is strange?"

"Not at all! It is quite common that all gods, goddesses; the ones that head the institutes , for senior guard members to fill in and cover each other when one is called out onto the field. She will simply say she is covering Madame Sinclair."

"Madame Sinclair?"

"Madame Sinclair is the usual Nephilim who tailors the female Nephilim Guard." Lola thanks Athena for her protection. Athena nods in acceptance of Lola's thanks as she exits the office.

*

Atticus and Athena are in their weekly past-life regression session in the computer room. participating in another past life session. Atticus looks around at where himself and Athena are. They are back in the woods, this time it is night. Atticus looks up at the sky. The sky is completely clear, he can see every star; to him it looked like the night sky had had glitter sprinkled all over it, it was mesmerising.

Athena looks up at the sky, following Atticus's gaze. "Beautiful, isn't it?" Atticus nods.

"Lola would want to lie on the grass and look at this all night, if she could," Atticus comments. Athena looks at Atticus brows furrowed.

"You have become quite attached to her." Atticus looks from the sky to Athena,

"Who?"

Athena smiles.

"Lola."

Atticus hears a man's voice yelling in the distance, and decides to follow it. Making his way through the long uncut grass, trees, and flowers, he stops when he spots a light from a campfire. Standing in front of the campfire was past-life him, and the Nymph woman he had seen before; during his first past-life regression. Not far from them stood another man, a dark-haired man like past-life him, olive skinned, but older, and round around his middle. Atticus hides behind one of the trees to spy on the trio.

"You do not have to hide, they cannot see us, we are not really here." Athena reminds him. Atticus looks over his shoulder at Athena, then turns his attention back to the trio around the fire. He keeps himself hidden behind the tree, ignoring Athena's comment about them not being able to be seen.

As he looks on at past him shouting at the man, the strange, rounded, older man pulls out a spear, aiming it at the beautiful wood nymph. Past him waves his hands around in the air, a beautiful golden instrument shaped like the letter 'U', around ten inches tall, filled with golden strings appears before him; it is an instrument that Atticus has never seen before. Past

-life him starts to play it. As he plays it, the most beautiful music Atticus has ever heard starts to come from it. The strange man with the spear goes into a hypnotic trance. Past him grabs hold of the beautiful Nymph's hand and yells at her to run.

Atticus hears a popping sound, and finds himself back in his own body, laying on the hospital bed.

"NO!" he shouts, he turns to Athena.

"Take me back! Now!" Atticus demands. Athena shakes her head.

"I cannot do that Atticus."

"Why?" he shouts. Athena looks at him sternly.

"You were becoming too caught up. I had to bring you out."

Atticus feels rage pumping through his veins. Athena places a hand on his shoulder. "Breathe, Atticus. Remember these are *past* life memories. What you are feeling, is what you felt during that memory. It has no relation to who you are now, who you are today. Look at me, Atticus." Atticus looks at Athena.

"Breathe," she says calmly. Atticus starts to take deep breaths in and out, breathing in through his nose, exhaling out through his mouth. He starts to feel the anger that had consumed him start to diminish.

"Good, Atticus, that's it, breathe. Release the anger. Good."

*

As Lola and Josiah walk towards Pentre Ifan, Lola asks Josiah where it is exactly that they are going, where is the tailor based.

"They are based on another institute near the Poulnabrone dolmen, in County Clare, Ireland." Josiah informs her. Lola stops in her tracks,

"Ireland? We're going to Ireland?"

"Yes Ireland, where all the Leprechauns are. That really is a myth, there is no such thing as Leprechauns. Why are we not moving?" Josiah edges Lola to move.

"I have never been to Ireland before," Lola says, continuing to walk towards the Pentre Ifan dolmen.

"County Clare is only a few hours' drive to the Blarney stone. We could ask Henri to drive us there, make a day of it. I am sure he wouldn't mind."

Lola smiles and overtakes Josiah on the path leading to the Pentre Ifan portal.

*

Henri answers the County Clare's Nephilim institutes main door wearing a woolly navy dressing gown. He reminds Lola of one of those men in old painted portraits of gentlemen in their studies, smoking a pipe, sitting in an old chair with their legs crossed, perched up on a matching foot stool, although, Henri is certainly not old. He is just how Lola remembers him, despite her tipsiness at the party. Tall, broad, like the brothers, maybe broader due to being slightly older, and therefore more filled out. Jet black hair, startling blue eyes, high cheekbones, and a chiselled square jawline. Lola thinks, although dishevelled and puffy eyed, you can still see that Henri is a very handsome man. Henri embraces Josiah with a warm, open hug.

"What's happened?" Josiah asks Henri as he continues

sniffles, he has clearly been crying. Lola has never seen a grown man cry before; she finds it refreshing.

Henri sniffs, pulls out a handkerchief from one of the dressing gown pockets and blows his nose.

"Alice and I broke up."

"What?" Josiah is shocked by this news.

"she says she wants to go away travelling for a year, alone. She thought it best we should have a break, explore new sides of ourselves, whatever that means. I am very well acquainted with all my sides already."

Henri steps aside allowing them both to enter, he closes the door behind them.

"Why are you here?" he asks them.

"Lola passed her assessments and needs to be measured for her Nephilim Guard gear." Josiah informs him. Henri smiles and embraces Lola in a hug, Lola deciding it best to ignore his snotty face, and just go with it, allows him to hug her.

"Congratulations, Lola! Welcome to the Nephilim Guard family!"

"Thank you, Henri. I'm happy to finally be joining you."

The institute's doorbell rings, Henri opens it, revealing Aphrodite. It was almost as if Josiah, and Henri had been taken over by body snatchers, they were completely awestruck.

"Lola, my love." Lola turns towards the sound of a foreign, possibly French accent. *'Ah! This must be Madame Sinclair.'* An extravagant lady dressed in an emerald green pencil skirt dress, and ruby red hair styled fashionably in the style of Marilyn Monroe is approaching them whilst putting on a matching emerald green jacket.

"I am sorry, I have to dash, Lola, an emergency has arisen,

and I need to go and assist. But I am leaving you in good hands, Aphrodite will be attending to your fitting today." Madame Sinclair kisses Henri, Josiah, Aphrodite, and Lola on both cheeks, before rushing out of the institute.

Henri and Josiah do not seem to have acknowledged the interaction between them and Madame Sinclair. Aphrodite wiggles her nose, instantly snapping Henri and Josiah out of their awestruck state. Lola laughs, as she watches them shake their heads.

"Hmm." Aphrodite says glancing down at Josiah with one raised eyebrow. Aphrodite kisses Lola on each cheek. "Well Miss Belmonte, shall we get started?" Henri assists Lola with taking off her coat. Lola follows Aphrodite down a long yellow and off white corridor.

*

Lola is standing in the middle of a fairly large room lined with clothes from all decades of time, Aphrodite sees her studying them as she is taking her measurements.

"They're in preparation for what Zeus foretold. We do not know for sure if anybody is going to fulfil the premonition, but we must be prepared in case it does happen. Since we do not know what time they might travel to, or who out of the Nephilim Guard will have to go, all institutes have a room like this one." Aphrodite walks over to a table that is placed underneath the windowsill and picks up a computer tablet like the one Rashida had during Lola's assessment and starts to type on it. "Your abilities? Apart from the special one I have been informed about?"

"Earth and Aquatic manipulation." Aphrodite inputs the

information onto the computer.

"Have we finished?" Lola asks Aphrodite.

"In a hurry?" Aphrodite replies.

"Josiah, Henri, and I are hoping to make the most of the day and take a road trip; I have never been to Ireland before."

"Yes, I have finished your fitting," Aphrodite says, answering Lola's question.

"Thank you," Lola says as she picks up her coat and bag.

"Lola!"

"Yes?" Lola says turning to face Aphrodite before she exits the room. Aphrodite walks over to her and kisses her on the cheek.

"A word of advice from the goddess of love herself. People do not always show how they truly feel, keep that in mind. Don't put all your eggs into one basket as the saying goes. There is going to come a point... soon, where you will have to choose between three different suitors. When faced with this decision, fully think about each one. Do not go with the choice that you think people will expect you to make, or you think is logical, or if you think you must choose them out of duty. Look deep in here." Aphrodite places her palm onto Lola's heart. "Examine how you would feel if you were to say yes to each of them, who you would feel the slightest bit of doubt with, pay attention to how each yes makes you feel. With one of them you will feel a sense of release, a lift from within you, choose that one. That is all, you may leave."

Chapter Five

By the time Josiah and Lola arrive back at the institute, Henri in tow. Athena, Atticus, and Markus were already finishing up dinner.

"Henri, I was not expecting you." Athena says upon seeing him. Henri walks over and kisses Athena on the cheek.

"I hope you do not mind, I needed to give myself some space from Poulnabrone." Henri takes a seat next to Atticus. Josiah and Lola seat themselves next to Markus and start to pile food onto their plates.

"Of course, I don't mind, you are welcome here anytime. Are you okay?"

"Alice and I broke up," Henri says informing her as he too starts piling food onto a dinner plate.

"Oh, I am sorry," Athena responds sympathetically.

"It's okay. I figured it might be a good thing. It may provide me with the space I need to discover new things about myself," Henri replies.

Henri glances over at Lola at the end of his statement. She sees, but dismisses it, carrying on eating the food piled on her plate. She remembers what Atticus had said to her the night he came to her bedroom, drunk, after her birthday party; about Henri always being the favourite. Although Lola cannot deny that Henri is handsome, as all male Nephilim appear to be, she currently has no opinion on him in connection to him becoming a crush of hers.

Atticus hands Lola a little wooden box.

"This came for you today. I think it's your weapon. They are usually delivered in boxes made of wood." Josiah takes the box from Atticus and passes it to Lola.

Lola feels like a child on Christmas day unwrapping her presents from Father Christmas. When she opens the lid, it reveals a ring, she holds it up to study it, it is beautiful. The ring has five gems in the shape of a Pentagon. One is a dark green and black marble stone, one is amber, another is a stone, the colour of the deep-sea blue. The last two are quite clearly ruby and sapphire. Athena holds out her palm, Lola passes the ring to Josiah, who passes it to Markus, who places it in Athena's outstretched hand. Athena takes the ring from Markus, studies it then continues to inform Lola what each stone is; what it represents. Starting with the green and black marble stone,

"Malachite, Earth; Citrine, Fire; Blue Opal, Water; Sapphire, Air; Ruby, Life." Athena smiles and hands the ring back to Markus, to pass back to Lola. Lola takes a closer look.

"Does it need to be placed on a certain finger?"

"Not particularly, we recommend the mortal wedding ring finger. It's the only finger that has a direct vein connecting to the heart, therefore, it makes its abilities stronger." Lola slides the ring onto her finger. Lola looks around the table, she has drawn the attention of all three Hardy men.

"What? Apart from Henri, you already know that my abilities allow me to call upon Earth, and Water. Maybe this means at some point I will also develop the ability to call upon the Air, and Fire elements too." Lola shrugs and carries on eating the remaining food from her dinner plate.

Athena rings the bell, minutes later Berty appears, carrying a tray of desserts, a cheesecake, and a strawberry and cream sponge cake. He places the desserts on the table in front of them and starts to clear up the finished dinner plates. Henri is the first to pick up the dessert knife and offers out the cheesecake to the other's.

"Thank you Berty, thank you Henri," Athena says as Henri slides a piece of cheesecake onto Athena's dessert place. "How did the fitting go, Lola? Did you have a nice day exploring some of the beauties of Ireland?" Henri slides a slice of the cheesecake onto Lola's plate as requested.

"Thank you Henri, and yes, Athena, Aphrodite made me feel very welcome, and comfortable. Henri was kind enough to drive Josiah and I to the Blarney stone."

"It sounds like you all had a fun day," Markus says smiling at Lola.

"Yes. Both Josiah and Henri spoilt me today, allowing me to drag them both around. Today I was a real tourist."

"Athena, may I please be excused?" Atticus asks, Athena nods, giving Atticus permission to leave the dinner table. Atticus stands and turns to face the others. "Sorry. Today has been a long day. I hear my bed calling me." Markus agrees with Atticus and asks permission to leave the table also. Athena smiles.

"Actually, I am feeling rather exhausted too. I hope you…" looking at Josiah, Henri, and Lola, "…do not mind if we all call it a night?" Henri stands.

"Not at all." He turns to face Lola. "Would you allow me to escort you back to your room?"

"But you are the guest, not me," Lola replies. Henri laughs.

"I have practically spent my whole life here, Lola. Trust me I am no guest."

Lola looks around at Athena, Markus, Josiah, and Atticus.

"Yes, all right, I don't see why not." Lola and Henri exit the room, following Atticus, Josiah, and Markus.

Once out of the room, Henri slows his walking pace, clearly allowing the brothers to walk ahead of them both, leaving them to fall considerably behind. Henri stops and faces Lola, he lifts Lola's finger, the one with the ring on, and points to the ruby.

"Lola, I know what this represents." Lola smiles.

"It represents life," Lola comments.

"Yes, but not just life, it represents blood. This gem is only placed in weapons where the Nephilim, whom it's made for, is a shapeshifter."

Lola pulls her finger away from his grip and looks down both sides of the corridor, making sure no one overheard Henri's comment.

"Do not worry, I will not tell anyone. Your secret is safe with me," Lola looks up at Henri and whispers.

"How did you know?"

Henri glances down to the right, as if trying to recall something.

"The brother's father was the first to discover it. When my mother; his sister, approached him for his help in finding something that could help her with her ability to shapeshift." Henri looks at Lola, "My mother possessed the shapeshifting ability. I know how that makes you a Nephilim of extreme interest, Lola. If that information fell into the wrong hands, I know how dangerous that could be for you, and anyone you care about. I give you my word, on my mother's soul, your secret is safe with me."

*

When Lola walks into the computer room for her first shapeshifting lesson. Athena is not alone, standing beside her stood Aphrodite. *'I wonder why Aphrodite is here?'* Lola thinks. As if Athena had just read Lola's mind, she answers her thoughts.

"Lola, Aphrodite has kindly agreed to be your test subject."

"My test subject?"

"Yes, shapeshifting into a human, is quite different than taking camouflage against a tree. When shapeshifting into another entity, you need a drop of their blood, or some of their DNA. Aphrodite has kindly agreed to be the entity you will be shifting into today. Shall we start?"

Aphrodite holds out her hand towards Athena. With a needle, Athena pricks Aphrodite's finger.

"Now you," Athena instructs Lola. Lola holds out her hand for Athena to take, she pricks the middle finger of Lola's right hand. Athena keeps hold of Lola's finger, Aphrodite places her pinpricked finger against Lola's, transferring her blood.

"Now, Lola, I want you to close your eyes." Lola does as Athena instructs and closes her eyes.

"I want you to picture Aphrodite. Focus on her every detail. Whilst keeping the image of her in your head, I want you to imagine a golden light slowly spreading through you; starting from your heart, spreading down your arms, down into your stomach, into your hips." A gasp escapes Aphrodite's mouth. Lola starts to feel her body fill with a warm glow, her fingers, her toes start to tingle.

The sound of Henri's voice through the door brings Lola out of the trance, the warm glow within her fades.

"I am sorry to interrupt, but Lachesis and Atropos are here to see you. They say it's urgent," Athena apologises, excuses herself and follows Henri out of the computer room.

*

Lachesis and Atropos are waiting for Athena outside of her office. On approach, Athena sees both sisters are anxious. They follow her into her office.

"Lachesis, Atropos, what has happened?"

Atropos biting on her bottom lip, is the first to speak.

"I overheard an argument, Clotho was having with her mortal lover. He was wanting to end the affair. Athena, she told him that she was going to make sure he was never born."

"Do you think she meant it? It sounds like a typical lover's quarrel to me," Atropos takes a step towards her.

"Athena, if we did not think she meant it, we would not be here." Athena gives Atropos an understanding nod.

"How do you think she will do this?" Athena asks the sisters. Lachesis takes out a piece of folded paper from her pocket, unfolds it and places it onto Athena's desk, it looks like a family tree, one of the names has a circle drawn around it. Athena studies the paper.

"What is this?" Athena asks. Atropos is the one to answer, pointing to the circled name.

"This is Alec's great grandmother. Her family was one of the families sent into the Warsaw ghetto in 1940. She was one of the children Irena Sendler saved. We believe she has, or is going to travel back, to Warsaw and prevent that from happening. If she was not rescued from the ghetto, then she would have been killed, therefore erasing Alec, his mother, and grandmother from existence." Athena continues to study the family tree.

"Do you know when she might have to travel to?" Athena enquires. Lachesis pulls out a notebook from her bag, opens it, and places onto the desk in front of Athena.

"It looks as if Clotho has been tracing back both Irena's and Stefan's lives, their relationship leading up to the ghetto before the Nazi's arrival in Warsaw. We think she is going to prevent the very beginning of Irena's mission to save the children."

"Which would be when?" Athena asks.

Lachesis replies, "We think Stefan showed Irena, the underground tunnels in 1942. He showed them to her because they were lovers. We have been tracking Clotho's computer; she has been researching their relationship, when, and where they first met. We think she is going to prevent their relationship from forming."

"How would she do that?" Athena asks.

"By getting to Stefan before him and Irena met, or before they became lovers." Athena folds up the paper, closes the notebook and gives them both back to Lachesis.

"Do you know when that might be?"

"We know they met before Nazi invaded Warsaw in September 1939. We think she would attempt to get him in enough time before that first meeting, a month or two before perhaps."

Athena presses a button on her communicator. Moments

later, Berty appears in her office.

"Berty, please fetch Atticus, Markus, Josiah, Lola, and Henri." Berty exits the office. Once Atticus, Markus, Josiah, Lola, and Henri had filtered into her office one by one, Athena asks them all to take a seat.

"Lachesis and Atropos have come to us with some villainous news. I am afraid Zeus's premonition might be about to come true." The Hardy men and Lola look around at each other anxiously. Athena continues to update them.

"Clotho is planning on travelling back to 1939, at least we think it might be 1939. She wants to prevent Irena Sendler from accomplishing her mission." The Nephilim in Athena's office look around at each other once more, Athena continues.

"We do not know when in 1939 she might be travelling to, only to where. Markus, I need you to assist me in gathering further information. Henri, I need you to take over Atticus, and Josiah's practical training, and Lola, from now on you will join them. You all should start preparing for your trip."

"Our trip?" Lola enquires.

"Markus has not yet healed from the poisoning of the dagger that cut him; Henri will be needed to assist Apollo in looking after the manor. Lachesis, Atropos, and I will join you, Atticus, and Josiah in Warsaw, but first we need to arrange a few things here."

Atticus puts up his hand.

"Yes, Atticus?"

Atticus puts down his hand.

"Who is Irena Sendler?" Atticus asks. Athena smiles.

"Irena Sendler was a Polish woman who helped two thousand five hundred Jewish children escape the Warsaw ghetto during the Second World War. Many of whom grew up to be very influential people within human rights, political rights; scientists, doctors." Josiah was next to put up his hand.

"Yes, Josiah?" Josiah puts his hand down.

"Just to confirm, you are sending myself, Atticus, and Lola to Poland, to 1939, to find, and capture Clotho?"

"That is correct. However, you will not be alone during the capture of Clotho, as myself, Lachesis, and Atropos will be alongside you. Madame Sinclair and Aphrodite will oversee fitting you with the correct period clothing. Markus and I will find the safest way for you to travel to Warsaw, from the nearest dolmen. Any more questions?" The Nephilim Guards all shake their heads.

"Good. Atticus, Josiah, and Lola please change into your training gear and meet Henri in the training room in half an hour." Atticus, Josiah, Lola, and Henri nod in understanding and exit Athena's office.

*

Since passing Lola's assessments the gods had decided to change the training gear. Before they were allowed to wear their own exercise clothing. Now however, we have to wear a uniform similar to the olive field uniform, but instead of olive it's dark grey. Instead of a leather combined with a material containing nano's, it's made of a material similar to spandex, except more breathable. Lola enters the training room, all three Hardy men stop what they're doing, look and stare at Lola. Suddenly she becomes aware of how close fitting to the body, the gear is. Her body is built to be voluptuous, she thought the training and the exercise would lead her to be less so, but all the toning up did was enhance her natural hourglass body shape, and the strength she has built. In all honesty she has never felt healthier, fitter, or happier with her body. However, in this current moment, with the three men staring at her, she had never felt more self-conscious of her voluptuous body shape.

Nine floor mats have been placed in the middle of the room, creating a large square. In the middle of the mats, stood Atticus, and Josiah. As Lola steps onto the mats, Henri follows. For the first fifteen minutes Henri has them running laps, doing burpees, touch knees, butt kicks, and arm swings. Next, he has them partner up with each other to practice self-defence moves, placing Josiah as Lola's partner first, Josiah playing the role of the attacker. As Josiah comes up behind her, wrapping his arms around her arms and chest, clenching his hands in front of her, she feels his warm breath on the back of her neck. His breathing is heavy from the warmup. His breath on the back of her neck causes the little hairs on her arms to stand up. She tilts her head back as instructed to cause a distraction, but instead of taking a step back, as an attacker would do on instinct, he pulls her in closer to him, tilting his head down, his warm breath breathing out into the side of her neck. Not playing his part, she stomps down onto his right foot as hard as she possibly can, which does the trick, he steps back allowing Lola to kick back towards his groin. But he ducks out of the way speedily and she misses. She turns to face him, placing her hands onto her hips.

"What was that?"

Lola's annoyance clearly amusing him. She turns back to face away from him.

"Again! Properly!" she demands. He comes up behind her, wrapping his arms around her. She tilts her head back, this time he steps back, allowing her to kick his groin. Luckily as part of the men's uniform, they have to wear Abdo guards. Although, after Josiah's inappropriate behaviour Lola wished that were not the case. The thought of Josiah's reaction might have been to her kicking him in the groin makes her smile to herself.

"What did I miss?" Lola looks up to see Atticus approaching them.

"Nothing, a funny thought is all."

Atticus smiles, his glorious wide, warm smile.

"We're swapping partners. I'm with you now." He informs Lola. Continuing with self-defence, Atticus too takes on the role of attacker, and in one swift movement Lola has her arm under his chin, her foot behind his leg, and his 6'1 body pinned to the floor. It had been a while since Atticus and Lola have been partners during a training session, her new found strength and ability to pin him down takes him by surprise. For a moment they forget where they are. As Lola looks down at Atticus lying on the floor beneath her, she feels her veins fill with a burning passion. A cough from Henri brings them back to the present moment. Atticus and Lola look towards Henri to find both, him and Josiah staring down at their intimate position.

"Lunch break?" Henri suggests before cheekily smiling at them, and turning to make his way towards the training room's doors to exit.

Chapter Six

The air is cool against Lola's skin; she looks up at the evening sky, it's filled with oranges and pinks, it reminds her of fire. Henri is sitting on the stone bench as she walks down the stone steps leading from the house into the garden.

"May I?" She asks Henri for permission to sit. Henri nods. Joining him in looking over the gardens, Lola finds herself studying his profile; his brow is strong, he has a roman nose, a square jaw line, a strong chin. His dark hair has grown longer since the party, and slight waves have started to take form. She looks back towards the gardens.

"What was she like?" Lola says attempting to make small talk with him.

"Who?" his voice is calm.

"Your mother. You, Josiah, Atticus, and Markus are not from this time, are you?" he looks at her, contemplating, she notices his eyes are the colour of the ocean. He bends his neck back to look up at the sky.

"No, we are not. We were born in France, in the sixteenth century. That is all I can tell you about where we are from, it's not my place to tell you of our history." Henri brings his neck back down to continue to look over the gardens. "My mother's name was Anne; she was the sister of the brother's father, Michel. We all lived together; she was a shapeshifter. The royal family had heard of her talents, but they were scared of her brother, we were under his protection. The morning after Michel's death, the royal guards came and took her and the brother's mother away. I never saw her, or my aunt again. I tried researching them both, but it appears neither of their whereabouts were ever documented."

"What was she like?" Lola asks him again.

"She was strong, brave, kind, loving and extraordinarily passionate. She would get excited over the smallest things, and she was always smiling and laughing."

"She sounds like a great woman." Lola feels Henri's eyes on her, studying her profile, as she had studied his.

"What about your mother? What was she like?" he asks Lola in return. She closes her eyes and tries to remember. An image of when she had fallen over; when she was six and had scraped her knee, it was bleeding. She was crying, her mother was demanding her to stop crying, because 'only babies cried'. Lola opens her eyes and looks into Henri's ocean-blue eyes.

"She was not like the other mothers I saw and met; She was blunt. She would hug me of course, but she wasn't very maternal in the sympathetic, compassionate sense. She was a warrior through and through. I guess, looking back, she was a guard member first, a mother and wife second. My Dad was and has always been the affectionate one. Now I see that to him; his duties as a father, always came first, being a member of the guard came second."

Talking about her mother and father made Lola's stomach fill with knots. Although her mother had not been the most maternal mother, she knew she loved her as much as she could have.

"I wonder if she were alive, what she would think of me. Would she be proud? How would she be talking to me about men. Would she be happy that I chose to become a member of the guard? Probably, as she herself always put being a Nephilim warrior first. Would she be a pushy mother with high expectations? Or, a supportive mother, support whatever choices I made?

"I wonder sometimes if she would be proud of me," She says opening herself up to him. Henri smiles a gentle, comforting smile.

"I wonder sometimes if my mother would be proud of me too. Ahh…" Henri runs his fingers through his hair. "I guess being part of the Nephilim guard isn't exactly the ideal career for living a long life."

"No different, if we were policemen, or firemen… women," Lola says. Henri chuckles.

"I guess not."

"But we have choices. We can take on other careers too if we wish. I plan on becoming an architect." Lola informs him, opening up to him more.

Henri, still smiling his comforting smile, says,

"True. Although I cannot imagine doing, being, anything else. For me being part of the guard feels like life, like electricity running through my veins. When I'm out there on the field, I feel alive."

As Lola looks back over the gardens, the sun is starting to set. One thing she dislikes about Winter, the sun sets early. She looks down at her watch, it's just after three thirty.

"Maybe paint." Henry continues to say. Lola looks at him, he is somewhere else.

"If I were to do anything else, I would be a painter."

I smile. Feeling someone's eyes on her, Lola turns to face the manor, as she looks up towards the library, both Josiah and

Atticus are looking down at Henri and her through one of the library windows. She turns her attention back towards the gardens. In a comfortable silence, Henri, and Lola continue to watch the sun set over them, and the fields beyond. She still had time before meeting her father for dinner.

*

Atticus continues to watch Lola and Henri sitting together in the garden. Josiah walks back over to the library table and sits, continuing to read one of the world histories books that are spread across it.

"Atticus, stop spying on the lovebirds, we need to find out more about Stefan and Irena's whereabouts. Come and read." Atticus sighs and takes a seat back down opposite his brother, his focus continuing to be on the window. Josiah looks up from the book he is reading, studies his brother, then continues to read.

"You should tell her."

Atticus looks at his brother reading.

"Tell who what?"

"Lola, how you feel about her. Instead of overthinking what is happening between her and Henri. Which is nothing because Henri is still besotted with Alice." Atticus pulls one of the books towards him and starts to read.

"I am not overthinking anything. I know, Henri. I just don't want to see Lola get hurt. She's a good friend."

"A good friend? Okay, brother, if you say so."

Various history books are piled high all over the table Empty cups, empty chocolate wrappers, crisp packets, and fruit peels are scattered, showing signs they have been

88

researching for hours. Josiah stands up in excitement and slides one of the books over to Atticus, pointing to a section.

"It's a published book of Stefan's diary. I have read this diary, and re-read it over, and over again. It has always mentioned Irena, never where, or how, or when they met, but look it has changed. I haven't read the name Celestyna before. Look at the date and then look at what it says."

7th August 1939

I heard today that my dear, loyal friend Filip has passed.

I discovered this when his wife Celestyna paid me a visit. I must say that she was not what I expected; she is young, and exceptionally beautiful.

I am wondering, would it make me a beastly friend if I were to ask her out for dinner?

"This Celestyna lady, I have not read her name before." Josiah picks up the diary and continues to flick through it. He comes to another entry mentioning Celestyna's name.

12 August 1939

I thought I would mention that I had decided to ask Celestyna to dinner, to which she said yes. We talked for hours.

Earnest has invited me to dinner at his and Lena's home. I am going to ask Celestyna if she would like to join me. I consider Earnest not only a valuable fellow Lawyer, but a true friend. I would like to introduce Celestyna to him. I feel things may develop further with her.

Josiah flicks back through the published diary.

"August seventh is the first entry with Celestyna's name.

Atticus, do you think it's possible that Clotho has already travelled, that she has taken the form of Celestyna?" Atticus stands, picking up the diary.

"I'm not sure. Wouldn't her sisters have felt it? Either way we must inform Athena of the diary changes."

Josiah follows Atticus out of the library. Atticus walks towards Athena's office.

"Atticus, she won't be in her office. It's almost time for dinner, she will be in the dining room." Atticus follows Josiah towards the dining room. Athena is setting the table, Lachesis, and Atropos teleport into the room landing either side of her. Atticus holds out the book. Athena looks between them all. Atropos is the first to speak.

"She's travelled."

"Stefan's diary has changed," Josiah informs her. Athena takes the book from him and reads the entries.

"August seventh is the first entry mentioning a new name, Celestyna. Do you know who the Filip is that he is referring to?, his friend that passed?" Josiah asks, Athena shakes her head.

"It is impossible to remember every living soul. I will call Zeus immediately and request to see the records. The records will inform us of Filip's connection to Stefan, of his life and his wife Celestyna. I will call Madame Sinclair and Aphrodite. Atticus, Josiah, locate Lola and meet them in the wardrobe room to be fitted in half an hour. I will call Markus and prepare your map from Earthen Long Barrows to Warsaw. You are to travel first thing in the morning."

*

When Lola passed her assessments and joined the 'Nephilim' guard, and became a full-time resident at the manor, she was worried how it would affect her father, first her mother passing, and now she had made the decision to leave him behind also. However, when she placed her key through the keyhole, opening the door to her childhood home, she was surprised to hear the sound of a woman's laugh.

"Dad?"

Alastair appears out from the front room and throws his arms around her, giving Lola the tightest hug, he had ever given her.

"Lola, what a lovely surprise! And excellent timing. There is somebody I have been wanting to introduce you to." She follows him into the front room. Sitting on the sofa is a woman, her ankles crossed. Lola recognises her from one of her father's old work Christmas party photographs. The lady is a plain but attractive, with a small heart shaped face, high cheekbones, and a look of Indonesian, or perhaps Korean. She has big round brown eyes, jet-black wavy hair, with a few stray grey hairs, with the length ending just below her shoulders. She's wearing a pair of smart, dark blue jeans and a blush pink blouse. Her face is friendly, warm, and open.

"Lola, this is Cecelia." Cecilia stands and shakes Lola's hand.

"Lovely to finally meet you, Lola. Your father talks about you non-stop."

"All good things I hope?" Lola looks at her father, his eyes are gleaming.

"Nice to meet you, Cecelia." She lets go of Cecelia's hand. Cecelia apologises for having to leave but she has a dinner date with some friends of hers. She picks up her bag, and Alastair escorts her to the door. Lola seats herself on the sofa, trying to eavesdrop on their goodbye. Moments later Alastair pokes his back into the room.

"Tea?" he asks.

"Of course!"

As Alastair is making her a cup of tea, she relaxes back into the sofa. Looking around the room everything is exactly the same, as it were before she moved to the manor.

Alastair enters the room and places her cup of tea on the coaster sat on the oak coffee table that stood in front of her.

"She seems nice. How long have you two been seeing each other?" Alastair relaxes back into his armchair.

"Is it that obvious?" he says, he's happy.

"The twinkle in your eyes as you look at her, gave it away."

"It's very early days, but it feels right."

Lola leans forward and places my tea on the coaster.

"Dad, I'm here because something has happened. The institute received a visit from Lachesis and Atropos. They think Clotho is planning on travelling back to Poland either during, or before the Nazi invasion. We have all been placed on high alert." Alastair smiles at her.

"Your first mission. How do you feel?"

She picks up her mug of tea, wrapping her hands around it.

"Excited, scared. Do you remember your first mission?"

"I remember it as if it were yesterday. It was how I met your mother. I never expected to be called upon to go out into the field. Not all guard members are. Although we all still receive a communicator, just in case. I was twenty-four and working in Coutts bank when my communicator bleeped for the first time. I was contacted by Apollo. When I returned the call, I was instructed to meet a fellow guard member and

92

Athena. The other Nephilim was your mother. When I first saw her, I thought she was beautiful, but she was quite a bit older than me. I thought I had no chance, I thought she was out of my league. She was the most fascinating woman I had ever met. We were both travellers, which is why it was us who were called upon. Our first travelling mission was to travel to France to the sixteenth century and assist Athena in rescuing siblings who had not yet come into their powers. Their mother had died, and their father refused to live as a Nephilim. He mistreated them, constantly beat them. It was our mission to rescue them from their father and hide them amongst a high-status Nephilim guard family." Alastair pauses for a moment to reflect before continuing on with his story.

"I was petrified, oh but what an adventure it turned out to be. To witness what it was like to live in another century, it was incredible. Lola, you were born to two Nephilim that were travellers, it's coming as no surprise that you are one too."

"Was that the only time you travelled?" Lola asks.

"No, there was another time also, after your mother had died. Do you remember that time I woke you up in the early hours, I took you to Fred's?" Lola nods. Alastair leans forward, his face serious.

"I am guessing you inherited your mother's shapeshifting ability too?"

"Yes."

"Lola, be careful. Shapeshifters are rare, and are highly sought after. Do not shapeshift unless it is absolutely necessary and only if you must. Make sure you are completely alone. Do not tell anyone. Does anybody else know, apart from Athena?"

Cupping her hands around her tea, she avoids her father's stare.

"Aphrodite, and Henri. Athena had to tell Aphrodite in order for my uniform to be made. Henri knew when he saw the ruby in my ring."

"Henri Hardy?" he enquires. Lola nods. Alastair strokes his chin.

"Hmm, his mother likely had a ring, or some other piece of jewellery that contained a ruby also. It is rare, but only shapeshifters know the Ruby is only worn by someone possessing the ability; it is a secret they take to their grave. He must have seen his mother change at some point, and guessed the gem was connected to that. Nephilim cannot wear gems, or stones, unless they are linked to their abilities, as each gem, or stone contains a high concentration of energy linked to many different things. After what happened to his mother, he likely knew why what happened to his mother. You may be able to trust him, but still remain cautious."

Lola's communicator beeps. She answers it.

"It's Atticus. I'm needed at the institute." Lola stands up and kisses her father on his cheek and squeezes him tight.

"Lola, you will be fine. The Hardy boys are the best Nephilim I have seen in decades, and Athena, well who can beat Athena?"

Lola feels a tear run down her cheek. She wipes it away.

"I know. I just don't like leaving you behind," she tells him. Alastair chuckles.

"Every bird needs to flee the nest at some point. I am so proud of you for following your heart. Passionate, strong, and brave just like your mother. She would be so proud of you." Alastair kisses her head.

Markus teleports in, taking them by surprise.

"Markus, I thought you were not fit enough to teleport?"

Lola asks him, concerned.

"I am for emergencies. Clotho has travelled, you're needed back at the institute to start preparing."

Lola gives Alastair, one last goodbye hug. Markus shakes his hand and she links her arm around Markus's arm and mouths 'I love you' to her father before they teleport out.

*

Lola arrives outside the wardrobe room and knocks. Madame Sinclair requests for her to enter. Atticus is folding one last item of clothing into an old brown leather suitcase and closes it, as she opens the door to enter.

"Thank you, Madame Sinclair," he says before picking up the case and exiting the room, squeezing past her.

"Lola." Madame Sinclair opens her arms to embrace her. "Let me have a look at you." She takes a step back, Madame Sinclair asks her to turn slowly, she does as she says. After studying her, Madame Sinclair turns to look through the clothes rails. The wardrobe room is a basic room, plain wooden flooring, wooden walls. Lola can tell as she looks up at the ceiling, and the wood supporting it, that this used to be the attic. The walls are lined with racks of clothing. Clothing separator hangers—each with a different time decade labelled on them—dividing the different styles.

Standing at the end of the room, is a stunning changing screen patterned with every colour you can think of. Madame Sinclair hands Lola some pieces of lingerie consisting of bras, girdles, and stockings.

"First underdress." Madame instructs, ushering Lola behind the changing screen.

95

Lola walks behind the screen and starts to change into the underdress pieces given to her. First the bra, then the knickers, the girdle and lastly the stockings. She wonders why lingerie changed; the items make her feel glamorous, feminine. Although the girdle is slightly loose around her waist, and the cup of the bra is slightly too small, she feels for the first time confident, sophisticated. She felt empowered.

"Let me see," She hears Madame Sinclair say. She steps out from behind the screen and lets Madame Sinclair check the fitting. Around her waist Madame Sinclair wore a black cotton apron filled with safety pins, a measuring tape, scissors, sewing needles and different coloured threads. She takes a safety pin and pins the gap of the girdle around Lola's waist, and walks over to the wooden chest of drawers that is placed below the attic window and pulls out another bra, for Lola to try on, and ushers her to the screen. She tries the second bra which turns out to be a perfect fit. She steps out from behind the screen to show Madame Sinclair. She places two fingers under the back of Lola's bra strap.

"Perfect." She walks over to one of the rails and hands Lola some skirts and blouses.

"You are curvier than the women in those days. The traditional hourglass body shape didn't come back into fashion until the 1950s. In 1930s, most women had a soft hour-glass body type. Therefore, clothes were not made to suit a traditional hourglass. I have given you bigger sizes to fit your bust and hips. I shall tailor your clothes to cater to your smaller waist."

Lola steps back behind the screen. Madame Sinclair was right, the clothes fitted Lola perfectly around her bust and hips, but then were too loose around her waist. Buttoning up her

96

skirt, Lola steps out from behind the screen. Madame Sinclair safety pins the items of clothing around Lola's waist, pulling the material in to fit. As Lola looks into the full-length mirror, she can't believe what she was seeing. The reflection in the mirror is no longer a reflection of a girl, but of a young woman. A young woman who appears elegant, sophisticated. The clothes complement and enhance her curves. She turns to view her profile; Madame Sinclair is stood beside her.

"What a beautiful young Nephilim warrior you are."

There is a knock at the door.

"Enter," Madame Sinclair instructs. Atticus enters and stands frozen staring at Lola.

"Sorry, I forgot one of my jackets."

Madame Sinclair continues checking the fitting of Lola's clothes.

"It's where you left it."

He doesn't move. Lola glances at Madame Sinclair through the reflection in the mirror, she stops checking her and passes Atticus his jacket.

"Is that all?"

"Yes, thank you." He nods and exits the room. Madame Sinclair continues to check the fitting.

"Okay, Lola. I think we are done. I know what you need. I will adjust the clothes and pack them into a suitcase for you. You will have them later tonight, ready for your departure tomorrow."

"Thank you, Madame Sinclair."

*

Apollo does not look how Lola expected him to look. In the

images she had seen of him, his hair was fair and wavy, his skin fair too. The man Athena introduces her to has hair that is dark, straight, cut short on the sides, longer on top, and his skin is tanned. On top of his right arm is a tattoo of the famous laurel wreath that is known to be his symbol. He is taller, broader, and bulkier than any of the Hardy men. When he speaks, his voice flows out smooth, velvety, like a symphony.

As he takes Lola's hands in his, a jolt of electricity shoots up through her arm. An image she had seen many times before in her dreams occurs. She's walking through a dark caved tunnel, the walls are cool, damp against her touch. She is not wholly there, she can feel the presence of others watching her, but she cannot see them, she can only see their shadows. Apollo lets go of her hands and she is pulled back to the present moment. Apollo, his smooth forehead has wrinkled by a furrow of his brows, he lets go of her hands.

"So, you are the famous Lola. My beloved sister keeps talking about you."

"Guilty as charged."

Apollo looks at Athena and raises an eyebrow.

"Ah, Atticus, Josiah good you are both here," Apollo says with a tone containing some amusement.

Atticus and Josiah throw their arms around him. Atticus squeezes his shoulder in a brotherly gesture before stepping back from him. Lola looks at the brothers in their 1930s menswear, it suits them, It's as if the 1930's fashion is what they belong in. Athena and Apollo walk over to a desk where Markus is standing studying a map of Poland. Atticus, Josiah, and Lola follows them. As Lola looks down and studies the map, she sees it's a map of what Poland was like during the time they will be travelling to, 1939.

"Let me explain your route. You will be arriving through

the Earthen Long Barrows Dolmen in Wiertrzychowice; it is roughly one hundred and eighty-seven miles to Warsaw; the Nearest city to Earthen Long Barrows is Tarnow." Markus points to a circle on the map.

"It's roughly twenty miles away. There you can find a public house where you will be able to stay the night. You will then be able to travel by train to Kielce." Markus points to the next circle on the map. "And then onto Warsaw. I will leave you to decide if you would like to stay the night in Kielce or wait half a day and catch a train to Warsaw, in which you will likely arrive around 22.30 hours." Athena hands them each an envelope.

"This should be enough to support you financially during your trip. Lachesis, Atropos, and I will meet you in Warsaw the day of the arrest to go through the plan. I shall send you a messenger with a place, and time. If you need to contact any of us at any point before then, press this button on your communicator." She points to a gold button addition. "It will connect you directly to Zeus, who will then be able to contact myself, Apollo, or Aphrodite. Markus will teleport you one by one to Alastair's. From there you will catch the bullet train to the nearest air station. Once in Poland, you will be greeted by a member of the guard named Alex. Alex will teleport you to Earthen Long Barrows. When you pass through the dolmen, focus on the date and time of when you would like to travel to. In this case, it would be nineteen hundred hours, August first, 1939. You will be arriving a week prior to Stefan and Celestyna's first meeting, giving yourselves plenty of time to travel to Warsaw. Any questions?" Athena says finishing up on their instructions Markus folds the map and hands it to Josiah; who places it inside one of the pockets of his jacket. Athena gives them all a goodbye hug one by one. Josiah is the first one

Markus teleports to Alastair's

*

When they arrive in Poland and walk through the arrivals gate, they are greeted by a fair-haired young man. Lola was used to male Nephilim being tall, taller than the average man, but this Nephilim is shorter. He is still broad, but not as broad as any of the Hardy men. When Josiah and Atticus see him, they freeze. Lola does not realise this until she reaches the man holding up the sign with their names written on it. She turns to face them. Atticus shouts his name in excitement, drops his suitcase, and jogs over to him, throwing his rms in the air and then wraps them around the fair-haired Nephilim.

"Pierre!" Josiah does not embrace him like Atticus but holds out his hand for him to shake, which the man takes happily.

"Alex, my name is Alex now. New time, new chapter, new start." Alex offers to carry Lola's suitcase for her, which she happily allows. Atticus and Alex walk ahead. Josiah and Lola follow behind, she looks at Josiah and mouths.

"Who is he?"

To which he simply replies,

"A very old friend."

She focuses her attention on Atticus and his old friend Alex, trying to hear any of the conversation that is taking place between them.

"And what about Adelice?" The tone in Atticus's voice when he said the name Adelice, his voice rung with affection. Alex looks down and shakes his head.

"I do not know. I have not seen her since that morning."

'That morning? To which morning was he referring too?'

100

She continues to listen.

"And what of you Pierre, Alex, when did you come?"

"Apollo brought me right after Athena brought you, your brothers and Henri."

"Why did you not reach out to me? I would have liked to have known that you were here, that you were safe."

"I wanted to forget," Alex simply says. Atticus nods in understanding and places his free arm around Alex's shoulders and squeezes his shoulder.

"I understand," He says, his voice lined with sympathy and compassion.

They follow Alex out of the airport, first he turns left, then right, then left again, leading them to a woodland area.

"We need to go deeper into the woods, just a little bit further, where the trees are able to hide us," Alex instructs. They continue to follow him deeper into the woods. He stops and looks around, checking that they are out of view from the general public.

"Who would like to go first?"

Josiah raises his hand and holds onto Alex's arm. Once Alex and Josiah teleport out, Lola turns to face Atticus.

"Who is Adelice?"

Lola has overheard him and Josiah mention her name before, but never asked any of them who she was. Atticus's reaction to seeing Alex, his reaction on hearing that this Adelice might still be alive, piqued her interest.

Atticus takes a step closer to her, their bodies an inch away from touching, he looks down at her, but then decides to take a step back to lean on to a nearby tree. As he leans back against it, he tilts his head back to rest on it and closes his eyes. Lola finds herself studying his face, his profile. She feels sadness spread throughout her; he looks to be in some kind of emotional turmoil. He tilts his head back to neutral, takes a step towards her, and looks intensely into her eyes.

"She was my best friend when I was child, back in France."

"Was that all?" she asks him curiously, trying to dig deeper. Atticus takes another step closer to her, again their bodies are an inch apart. They continue to look in each other's eyes, the electricity between them intensifies.

"Yes," He softly says. "We used to say that when we are fully grown, we would marry." He takes Lola's hands in his. "Just like childhood best friends sometimes say. But we were children." Atticus wraps his arms around her, embracing her, tighter than he has ever done before. They hear a pop, Alex has returned, they speedily step away from each other. Lola picks up her suitcase and links her arm through Alex's arm, the feeling of being sucked into air fills her, and then they land at the Earthen Long Barrows dolmen, where Josiah is waiting. Minutes later he teleports Atticus in. They thank him. Atticus, Josiah, and Lola pick up their suitcases, link their arms. As they take a step closer to the dolmen, a radiation of warmth, and feeling of calm project over them. As they step closer, they start to hear a ringing. Lola glances at Atticus, and then at Josiah, golden rays of sunlight beam out from the dolmen over them. The golden rays make the brothers look beautiful. Lola turns to face the dolmen portal ahead of them, they step through.

Chapter Seven

Earthen Long Barrows, 1939.

It was unexpected, that there would be a member of the guard waiting for them on the other side, in 1939.

"Hello, I'm Kevin," the handsome gentleman says, introducing himself. He is roughly six feet two inches tall, black hair, athletic, late 30's. Atticus, Josiah, and Lola look at one another, Lola is the first to speak breaking the awkward silence,

"Athena did not tell us that somebody would be waiting for us on the other side?" Kevin holds out a hand, offering to take Lola's suitcase.

"It was a last-minute suggestion. Zeus informed Athena that the Nazis have already started to invade Poland. They sent me because I am a teleporter. My instructions are to teleport you all to Tarnow, well, as near as possible. There is a public house there called The Wild Boar—which is located not too far from the centre of Tarnow—it is surrounded by tall trees, that will be able to hide our arrival. It is there Athena would like you all to stay the night."

Josiah is the next to speak,

"How do we know that we can trust you? That you're not a spy, working alongside Clotho, or the S.G.E.?"

Kevin glances at Lola.

"Do you think a great-great-grandfather would want to

harm his great-great-granddaughter?"

"That does not answer our question," Atticus says. Kevin, Lola's new claimed great-great-grandfather, takes his attention away from Lola and onto Atticus, pressing a button on his communicator. A second later, a projection of Zeus appears, he speaks in a deep, smooth voice.

"Atticus, Josiah, Lola. I am pleased to see that you have passed through into 1939 safe and unharmed. I have sent Mr Haim, Lola's great-great-grandfather to help assist you on your travels. Please follow his instructions. I will be keeping my eye on you." And on that, the projection of Zeus' face vanishes. Kevin picks up Lola's suitcase and holds out his arm for her to take. She looks between Josiah and Atticus, then wraps her arm around her great-great-grandfather's arm, he teleports Lola to a wooded area in Tarnow.

*

Kevin landed Lola amongst trees. Through an opening, Lola can make out an old, cobbled stone road, and a public house with a sign with the image of a red boar on it hanging on the wall above its main entrance. The public house looks old, possibly a building that was built during the late sixteenth century.

Lola hears the familiar popping sound of teleportation behind her. She looks over her shoulder to see Atticus and Josiah linking arms with Kevin.

"This is where I must leave you all," he informs them. Atticus and Josiah unlink their arms from his. Before they have the chance to thank him, he teleports out.

The Wild Boar is empty when they enter and make their

way to the bar to enquire about rooms.

"How may I help you?" says a buxom woman with brown ringlets pinned up and piled high on the top of her head. Josiah leans in towards her, switching on his charm.

"Three of your loveliest rooms, for one night please."

"You're in luck." The barmaid looks around the bar, and leans in towards Josiah, eyeing him up and down.

"Three *single* rooms?" She turns her glance towards Lola then back towards Josiah. He smiles.

"Yes, single," Josiah informs her. The barmaid smiles, bends down behind the counter, reappearing with three sets of keys.

"How many nights?" The barmaid asks, confirming the number of nights needed. Atticus is next to speak.

"Just the one." Atticus re-confirms.

"That will be twelve Zloty."

They take out the money envelope that Athena had given them and each hand the barmaid four Zloty. "Kristoff," she yells. A short, round, older man appears behind the bar next to her.

"Please show these lovely customers rooms two, five, and seven," The barmaid instructs, Kristoff nods, they thank the barmaid and follow Kristoff to their rooms.

*

Lola's room is made up of one single wooden chest of drawers, one single bed with simple plain sheets, and one blanket. She turns and thanks Kristoff for showing her to the room. Closing the door behind her, she places her suitcase down and walks over to the small rectangular window and looks out over the woods. She hears a knock on her door.

"Enter."

She turns to find Atticus standing in the doorway, holding the book she had asked him to pack into his suitcase, due to her running out of space in her own; women's 1930's clothing takes up quite a bit more room than men's clothing, she had discovered. He holds up the book.

"I thought you might want this back," he says presenting her with the book. She walks over to him, thanks him and invites him in. He looks around the room, "Maybe later. I want to have a wash and change into some fresh clothes before we have dinner."

"Good idea. Have you and Josiah discussed dinner timings?" she places her hand over her stomach.

"My stomach has been grumbling like crazy."

"No. Not yet, but..." Atticus looks at his watch. "I'm sure it won't take too long to wash up and change. We can meet you downstairs in around forty-five minutes?"

"Excellent!"

Atticus pauses for a moment looking at her, before smiling, tilting his head forward in goodbye, and making his way back to his own room.

*

When Lola enters the bar, Josiah and Atticus are already there. Josiah is wearing a light blue shirt, and dark grey trousers; Atticus is wearing a white shirt, with dark grey trousers also. Both of them look extremely handsome. Lola has chosen to wear one of the evening tea dresses in olive green and some stockings that have seams running up the back of them. Atticus and Josiah stand up on her approach, Josiah pulls out a chair that was placed between them for her to sit. As she steps in front of the chair, she notices Atticus staring down at her calves, where the seams from the stockings are on show. She sits down on the chair, Atticus and Josiah follow suit, sitting back down onto their own chairs. Lola can still sense Atticus's eyes on her lower calves, knowing exactly what he is thinking about. Although, she pretends she hasn't noticed his staring at her stockings. She looks around the bar, the experience feels surreal. Lola was in a bar, in Poland, in 1939. The architect in her is bursting to go outside and explore the buildings in the surrounding area. Whilst looking outside her room's window earlier that day, Lola noticed just beyond the public house's garden, there is a footpath leading to some buildings, including a church.

"Are we allowed to go out and explore?" she enquires. The barmaid approaches them, clutching a notepad and pencil.

"Today we are serving stew, with home grown vegetables and dumplings." Josiah flashes her his most flirtatious smile.

"Sounds delicious. We shall have three, along with two straight Vodkas and one Vodka with your freshly squeezed orange juice." The barmaid smiles and heads into the back, where they assume is where the kitchen is located.

"I assumed you would prefer Vodka and Orange rather than Ale or Vodka straight?" Josiah comments.

"You assumed right. So? Are we allowed to go and explore?" Lola enquires again. Atticus looks at his brother before answering her.

"Yes, as long as we go together, and don't interact with anyone." A grins appears across Lola's face.

"I saw a beautiful church that I would love to go and

explore in the town on the other side of the garden. I know we will not be able to go in, but we would be able to study the church's architecture from the outside. Can we go after dinner? Or maybe first thing in the morning, before catching our train to Kielce?" The barmaid reappears with their drinks and stews, placing them on the table before them. Josiah answers Lola's question once the barmaid leaves them.

"I think, it would be best to go first thing in the morning, rather than tonight. Since it is already getting dark, and I am sure you would like to get a decent night's sleep before our journey tomorrow to Kielce?"

Josiah is right, it has already started to turn dark, and Lola was feeling tired, also with the Nazis already starting to make their way into the Polish cities, first thing in the morning would be safest.

"Okay. First thing in the morning it is. But are we able to sit in the garden? It's a lovely evening. It would be a shame to not take advantage." Atticus is the one to answer Lola's question this time.

"Yes. The garden should be okay." He smiles and places his hand on top of her hand that was resting on her leg below the table, although it feels more like a comforting gesture, rather than a romantic one. She takes her hand from under his and picks up her drink. Lola doesn't like to play games, and so far, all Atticus has done is give her mixed signals. Until he makes it clear, and tells Lola how he feels, she thought it better to remain cool. Next to her she hears a quiet release of breath escape him, a silent sigh.

*

In the garden, there is a set of chairs sat next to a wooden, round table. On the table is an old oil lamp. Lola takes a seat placing her book onto her lap. She shuts her eyes, takes in a deep breath of the evening air, almost into a mediative state. She can smell the greenery, the trees, feel the warmth of the evening air against her skin. It reminded Lola of this one time when her parents took her to Florida, the air felt humid, like when a storm is approaching. She hears unfamiliar footsteps approaching her, she opens her eyes to see the barmaid approaching her.

"I saw you out here alone. I wanted to ask you about the young gentlemen that accompany you. Are any of them a suitor of yours?" 'A suitor?' It takes Lola a moment to understand what the barmaid meant, she is asking her if any of them is her partner. Lola shakes her in answer to her question.

"No. None of them are suitors. They are both single, as far as I know."

A smile spreads across the barmaids face. Of course, she has taken a fancy to both of them, they are both extremely handsome and charming. Lola feels a twinge of jealousy, within the pit of her stomach over the thought of another woman being attracted to them. More so, another woman that is beautiful and confident enough to make her attraction known. If anything were to happen between her and either Atticus, or Josiah, Lola knew she would only have herself to blame for not being confident enough to make her attraction known openly.

When Lola hears another pair of footsteps approaching, she peers around the barmaid to see Atticus. The barmaid smiles.

"That narrows it down." she winks at Lola.

"I shall leave you two alone."

On that the barmaid makes her way back into the pub. Lola picks up her book from her lap and opens it. Atticus takes one of the empty seats next to her.

"It appears you and your brother have picked up another admirer." Lola watches him looking around the garden from the corner of her eye.

"You were right, it is a lovely evening," he says making small talk. She places her book back down onto her lap and glances him; the moonlight shining onto his face, highlighting the shape of his masculine, angled face. She joins him in looking around the garden.

"It is." she smiles peacefully.

"What are you thinking about?" he asks her.

"Just how surreal this last year has been. A year ago, I was completely unaware of the Nephilim, that the gods, and goddesses were real, and now here we are in another time, Nephilim warriors ourselves. A lot has happened in such a short amount of time, it feels like it happened in a moment." A stray hair is covering one of her eyes. Atticus pulls his chair closer to hers and slides the strand of hair away softly using his fingers. Lola turns to face him, he looks intensely into her eyes, and starts to lean into her, tilting her face up towards his with his hand. He leans in further towards her and starts to tilt his head slowly to the right, just as Lola starts to do the same.

"There you two are!"

Upon hearing Josiah's voice Atticus drops his hand, and Lola opens her eyes. They lean back into their chairs and turn to face Josiah.

"That crazy barmaid came to my room, attempting to seduce me." He stops in his tracks, when he realises, he interrupted something between them.

"Was I interrupting something?" he says, noticing their startled faces. He continues to walk towards them and pulls out the third chair, taking a seat next to Atticus.

"Not at all," Atticus says, placing his hand onto his brother's shoulders in a welcoming gesture.

"The barmaid seems lovely. You should have taken her up on her offer," Atticus comments.

"She is lovely, you are right, but not as lovely as our dear Lola here." Josiah takes Lola's hand in his and kisses the back of it, she pulls it back.

"We need to discuss the plan for tomorrow" Atticus says.

"What time is the train?" Lola asks.

"Eleven forty-five" Atticus replies.

"Eleven forty-five a.m.?" Lola looks towards where she had seen the church, it could be no more than a few minutes' walk, via the footpath she had seen.

"Do we know how far the church is from the station?"

"I asked the barmaid. She says the church is opposite the station," Josiah replies. Lola tries to work out the timings in her head '*How long do I think I would need at the church? thirty minutes should be sufficient*'.

"Maybe we should leave around ten thirty, or just before? That should give us plenty of time to wash, dress, eat breakfast, make our way to the church, and leave in time to catch the train."

Josiah looks at Atticus. When they look at each other, Lola imagines them talking to each other telepathically.

"Ten thirty it is," Atticus says. Suddenly Lola feels extremely tired, she stands up, Josiah and Atticus stand also, she gestures for them to sit back down.

"I am suddenly very tired. I will see you both in the morning, breakfast at eight forty-five?" The brothers nod in agreement. As she walks away, she glances over her shoulder, Josiah has moved himself closer to Atticus, leaning into him, clearly making sure Lola cannot hear what he is saying.

*

The footpath leading to the church led through the woods. As they make their way through, Lola can't help but admire the beauty of the trees and flowers that surround them. She starts to hear beautiful music, what sounds like a harp playing in the distance. As they grow closer to the church, the trees start to appear taller. Lola looks up to see if she can see the sky, but all she can see are the tops of the trees. She turns her attention back to the brothers, who are walking just ahead of her.

The music from the harp starts to grow louder. As it does, the woods around her start to spin, she starts to feel herself fall. She opens her mouth to call to the brothers to stop, but no sound escapes her mouth. She opens her eyes to find herself lying face down on the ground of the woods, but it's night-time. She pulls herself up onto her hands and knees. She looks around to find the brothers, but they are nowhere to be seen. Lola's ankle feels sore, as she looks down, she sees blood, suddenly she feels the woods spin around her again. The sound of Atticus's warm, soothing voice is calling to her.

"Lola, Lola." Lola opens her eyes to see both Atticus and Josiah on their knees beside her, peering down at her.

"What happened?" Lola mumbles. She feels confused, disorientated, just a moment ago it was night and now it's daytime again.

"We didn't see what happened," answers Josiah. He continues,

"We were walking ahead of you when you started to shout 'Stop'. As we turned around, we saw you fall. Did you trip?" Lola glances down at where she had seen the blood dripping, but nothing was there. She looks back up at the brothers.

"I must have tripped." The brothers help her up and continue to support her, by supporting her arms.

"Are you okay?" Atticus asks her. Lola looks back down at her ankle, again nothing is there, but she can still feel the soreness.

"I'm fine. Just a bit shocked. I have never blacked out before." She detangles herself from their support, picks up her suitcase, and continues to walk along the footpath, limping. Atticus comes up from behind her and takes her suitcase from her grip. She stops and looks at him holding her suitcase.

"I can…"

Atticus interrupts her before she finishes her sentence.

"I insist," Atticus says to her in a 'matter of fact' tone. She looks at Josiah for back-up but he clearly agrees with Atticus's gesture. She looks back at Atticus's determined face.

"Okay. The train journey to Kielce will give me plenty of time to recover. I shall take it back then."

As Lola looks ahead, she can see the church steeple start to appear from above the treetops up ahead.

"Are you sure you're okay?" Josiah asks her again. She ignores him, keeping her focus upon the church steeple.

"Lola, you're limping. I think you should let me take a look," Josiah insists.

"My ankle is fine. It's probably just bruised from the fall."

"Still, it would make me feel better, if you would allow

me to take a look."

Lola lets out a deep sigh of defeat.

"Very well, if it would make you feel better." Josiah calls for Atticus to support her whilst Josiah checks her ankle. Luckily, the stockings she had decided to wear today are natural, therefore Josiah is able to see her ankle, and whether or not any bruising has occurred. As he examines her ankle, it appears dainty in his large, rough masculine hands. She notices Josiah's nails are short, bitten. She has never noticed him biting his nails. He presses his thumbs around her ankle bone, feeling for any swelling, then moves her foot up, down, and around.

"How does this feel? Any twinges? Any shooting pain, or dull aches?" he asks her. She shakes her head.

"Nope, none, and there doesn't seem to be any swelling or bruising," she states. Josiah frowns and looks up at her.

"I told you, it is fine. I am probably limping as a result of shock."

"Hmmm," he says and stands back up.

"Still best to keep an eye on it. Sometimes injury symptoms do not appear until an hour or so later."

"I promise to tell you if I do feel any twinges, pain, or aches," Lola reassures him.

*

Lola fall has put them behind schedule, therefore her time exploring the church, which turns out to be a cathedral, is reduced considerably. She barely has ten minutes to explore the beautiful gothic style cathedral, which looks fifteenth century, although it clearly has had some work done to it and studying the architecture the added work looks nineteenth century. However, the neo-gothic architecture is stunning. When Atticus, and Josiah say they have to leave, Lola feels angry with herself for blacking out and falling, leading them to have less time to explore the Cathedral.

The train to Kielce departs Tarnow on schedule. The train is a locomotive train, it is long, the metalwork has been painted red. The carriages remind Lola of the inside of an old American school bus. The middle aisle is narrow, and the seats are made up of benches that face each other, they are covered in ruby-red coloured leather. Lola takes a seat next to the window, facing forward. She had discovered during a day trip once with her father, that if she sat facing backwards on a train, she suffered from severe motion sickness. Josiah sits opposite her; Atticus decides to seat himself next to her. As Lola looks at the scenery of Poland passing them by, her eyes start to drift shut.

She looks ups at the clear, bright blue sky, the clouds are cumulus clouds. Lola learnt the names when she was a child. Her parents had bought her a little computer that came with cards, cards which you had to slide into the computer, and the computer would then ask you questions about what was on the card. The clouds used to be her favourite card. It's fascinating what sticks in your mind from your childhood.

Lola is standing at the top of a stone garden staircase. She gazes across the garden. The garden is filled with people in party wear, she takes to admiring their outfits whilst Atticus is at the garden bar grabbing them some drinks. Amongst the party guests, she notices a young boy running through the crowd towards the steps, towards her. As he approaches the steps, she sees the young boy is Atticus; *How could this be?* Lola realises she is dreaming. Atticus looks five or six years of age, he is wearing a long, white night shirt finishing at his

115

ankles. He stops on the steps before her, panting.

"I don't have much time," he says, panting between words from the running.

"I have to tell you."

"Tell me what?" Lola glances around at the party guests; she notices some women surrounding Atticus at the bar. Child Atticus follows her gaze.

"They do not mean anything to me. You have to listen to me. I am running out of time." Lola looks back at child Atticus's face as he continues to deliver his message.

"I saw you being born. I saw you as a child, and then I was born. I have seen you with our son and daughter." He holds out his hand towards Lola, reaching out trying to grab her, trying to hold on.

"No matter what happens, don't give..." Before he finishes delivering his message he fades away. Lola looks over at adult Atticus, who is still surrounded by admirers trying to catch his attention as he is still waiting to be served, he sees her face. He can tell she has just seen something. Leaving the bar, he walks over to her, takes her hand, and leads her to what appears to be a greenhouse, or a conservatory. He pulls out of one of the metal chairs from around the metal table and instructs Lola to sit. He pulls out the chair next to her and sits. He pours her a glass of water and places the glass in her hand.

"What did you see?" he asks, leaning into her. She looks up at him.

"You. You as a boy." Lola makes the choice not to tell him What child him said to her.

"You wanted to tell me something, but before you could deliver your message, you vanished." A tear starts to roll down Lola's cheek. Atticus takes the glass out her hand, and pulls her head towards his, resting their foreheads on each other.

116

"Why am I so weird?" she says to him under her breath.

"You are not weird. You have a gift." He kisses her forehead. She lifts her lips to his and kisses him, he pulls away.

"I'm sorry. I shouldn't have. I know we can't."

"Lola. Lola." Lola can hear Atticus's voice in the distance and starts to feel as if someone, or something pulling on her. She hears him calling her name again. "Lola." As Lola's feels her eyes slowly start to open, she can feel a hand upon her shoulder, a familiar hand that sends a familiar warmth throughout her. She opens her eyes fully to find herself looking straight into Atticus's chest. She sits up startled, he smiles.

"We are here." Lola looks out of the window to see the sun has set. She can just make out the sign stating that they were indeed now in Kielce.

Stepping out of the station, they turn right, to start walking towards the public house that Markus had showed them on the map, back at the manor. Kielce is completely different to Tarnow. The buildings are older and there are more vagabonds. Atticus suddenly grabs Lola's arm and pulls her into a side alley. As he ushers her to hide behinds the large rubbish bin, he places his hand over her mouth, signalling for her to remain silent, he removes his hand, she looks around to see if she can figure out an exit route. Lola notices the alley they are currently hiding in also opens up to another part of the town. Lola hears a large vehicle pull up along the entrance into the alley, and then a pair of heavy footsteps approaching them. A man starts to shout in their direction, his voice heavily layered with a German accent.

"I saw you hide young man. Come out with your hands behind your head and we will not shoot." Atticus looks at his brother and shakes his head. Josiah does what the Nazi says and walks out from behind the rubbish bin. Lola cannot see the

117

Nazis, only hear them.

"What are you doing out after curfew?" One of the Nazi soldiers asks Josiah. She can just make out Josiah's body profile.

"Sir, I have just departed the train that came in from Tarnow, I was on my way to the public house down the street, hoping I may be able to stay there the night, before carrying onto Warsaw tomorrow," Josiah informs them.

"Show me your papers," the Nazi demands.

"My papers are in my luggage, Sir," he answers. The Nazi soldier must have nodded and given him permission to collect his suitcase. As Josiah bends down to pick it up, he glances at Atticus and Lola hiding and winks at them in reassurance, that he is okay.

"Hurry!" the Nazi demands. Lola hears the click of Josiah's suitcase. Josiah hands over his papers to the taller one out of the two Nazi soldiers.

"I must ask you to come with us, so we can confirm that your documents are not fake." she hears the shutting of Josiah's suitcase, and his and the Nazi soldiers footsteps walking away from her and Atticus, and then the sound of the Nazi's turning on their engine, then the sound of the Nazi vehicle driving off with Josiah in tow. Atticus stands up and starts to chase after the Nazi vehicle, Lola follows, he stops when they're no longer insight and turns to face her.

"Josiah!" his voice is shaky. Atticus takes Lola's hand

"We must get to the public house as soon as possible. There we will be able contact Zeus without being seen."

118

Chapter Eight

Kielce, 1939.

Atticus and Lola enter the public house. It is vastly different from the one they had stayed in previously, in Tarnow. The first thing they notice is that it is full. Atticus squeezes her hand tighter, leading her through the crowds behind him, on the bar is a bell. Atticus rings it, an older stocky man comes to attend to them.

"We would like two rooms please. For one night." The man looks between them both.

"I am afraid we only have one room left, a double." he informs them. Atticus looks down at Lola, she looks at the barman.

"If that is all you have, then we have no choice but to take it," she says with assertiveness. Atticus bends his head down towards her and whispers into her ear.

"Are you sure?"

"The gentleman says that is all they have. I don't see we have any other choice?"

"Will you be taking it now or not?" the barman asks them.

"We will," Lola replies. The man opens a drawer behind the bar and hands them a key.

"Room 11. Pay on checkout. Through that door, straight up the stairs. Your room will be on the right."

*

"Lock the door." Atticus demands Lola as they enter their room. The room is more basic than the one in Tarnow. All it consists of is one double bed, which is set against the west wall of the room. There are no chest of drawers, no wardrobe, and the building is old and not well supported. Cracks are running all over the walls and there are damp stains on them as do the floorboards . As soon as Lola closes the door, Atticus presses the button that connects them directly to Zeus. Zeus' head appears.

"Atticus, Lola," Zeus says, addressing them.

"Zeus, upon our arrival in Kielce, Josiah was taken by the Nazis. We need Athena. We are staying at the public house here, the one suggested. We are in room 11. Please send help!"

*

Whilst the Nazis are checking Josiah's documents, they imprison him in one of the holding cells. From what Josiah can gather, the cell that he is being kept in is underground. There are no windows, and the walls are made up of grey, damp stone. They remind him of the manor, the passageway that leads from the library to the computer room. The thought sends shivers up and down his spine.

After what feels like hours, Josiah hears a knock on the cell bars, it brings Josiah out of his thoughts. The two Nazi soldiers that had brought him there are standing outside.

"Follow us," The shorter of the two soldiers instructs. Josiah gets up from, what he could only describe as a camping bed, and follows the soldiers to a room. As he enters the room, the walls—just like in the cell—are made of stone and are damp. In the centre of the room is a table. Two chairs are placed on one side of the table is a lone chair; *'This must be the interrogation room.'*

"Sit," the taller of the two soldiers instruct him. He does as the soldiers requests, and seats himself on the single seat opposite the two chairs. The two soldiers take the seats opposite him. The one who asked him to sit is holding a folder, he places it on to the table and opens it. He slides a photograph over to Josiah.

"This man was reported missing two weeks ago. Do you know him?" the shorter one asks Josiah. He leans forward to look at the photograph. The photograph is of a man wearing dungarees, a short-sleeved light grey shirt. He is wearing a flat cap, a handsome man, roughly in his mid-20s.

"No, sorry."

"Are you sure?" Josiah looks at the photograph again; he doesn't know anybody from this time, he plays along, he looks up at the soldiers.

"I'm sure," Josiah says again. The taller soldier looks at his colleague, and places Josiah's identity papers onto the table, along with another document. The taller soldier is next to speak. He points to his papers and then the certificate.

"Can you explain how your identity papers, and the details on it, match this man's birth certificate?" He points to the photograph.

"You do not look like the man in this photograph." *'Silence'* Josiah keeps him calm.

"It is possible that more than one Jakub Nowak was born on the seventeenth of November 1921. Unfortunately, my parents were not very imaginative." He stares the taller soldier out, keeping his cool.

121

"Were?" the taller soldier remarks. Josiah places his hands on the table and looks down at them; *'taking on submissive body language will make me appear vulnerable to them.'* Josiah thinks, reassuring himself.

"My parents were killed in an accident. My guardian growing up, was my aunt, my father's sister." he informs them.

"And what is your aunt's name?" the shorter soldier asks. Josiah thinks back to when Athena told them what name she was going to use during this mission.

"Magdalena Nowak. She shall be here soon, that's if your colleague rang the telephone number that I provided you with upon my arrival here."

The taller Nazi stands up, leans forward into Josiah's personal space and looks him dead in the eye, attempting to be intimidating him; *'I know my rights, they cannot do anything without sufficient evidence that my papers are not real.'* Josiah stares back at him. The soldier nods at his colleague, they both grab Josiah by the arms and pull him out of the room, down the corridor they came from. But instead of turning right towards Josiah's allocated holding cell, they turn left, and enter a room containing a large window. They force him to look through it; he gasps, and looks away, the taller soldier forces his head to look. On the other side of the window is another stone room, in the middle of the room stands a medical bed, positioned flat. On the bed is a prisoner, his clothes dirtied, his face stubbled, his face and body bloodied, his wrists are handcuffed to the frame of the bed. Standing at the bottom of the bed is a soldier. The soldier is flogging the soles of the prisoners feet with a thick leather belt, on the belt is a large buckle. The window has been sound-proofed, which blocks out the prisoners screams. The amount of blood dripping from his soles is immense. The tallest Nazi soldier brings his mouth close to Josiah's ear and softly says under his breath,

"If we find out that you are lying; that will be you."

*

As Lola lays on her side facing away from Atticus, she starts to doubt the decision she had made about them sharing a bed, maybe she should have let him stay on the floor. Lola looks at the floor noticing the thick layer of dust that sat upon it; no, she had made the right choice not to force Atticus to sleep on the dusty floor. It would have been selfish, mean even. She turns on to her back, letting out a deep sigh; one thing for sure, she will not be getting much sleep tonight. Lying beside Atticus, feeling him so close to her, the tension between them continuing to send waves of electricity through her, she lets out another sigh.

"Can't sleep?" she hears him mutter. She turns on her side to face him.

"I can't stop thinking about Josiah, do you think he's okay?" Atticus turns on to his side to face her, propping himself up on his elbow.

"Josiah is clever, strong, and the Nazis will find no reason to accuse him of anything incriminating. Athena will be here tomorrow; she will have a plan, and then we will get him back. Do not worry." Atticus returns to laying on his back. *Silence.*

"Atticus?"

"Yes?"

"Are you sleepy?" Silence, and then he sighs. "I was, but not so much now."

"Will you tell me about what happened with your

family?"

"What would you like to know?"

"Everything. About your parents, what happened to them. How Athena saved you. Unless that would make you feel uncomfortable, I understand if it would." she places her hand on his chest, for a moment it rests on his chest alone; until he places his hand upon it. Whenever he placed her hands in his, it felt natural, like that's where they belong.

"I don't mind. Where would you like me begin?"

"From the beginning. From when you and your brothers were born."

"Okay."

'*I wonder what he would do if I placed my head on his chest?*' Lola takes the risk and places her head onto his chest; for a moment he freezes beneath her, his heart starts to beat faster, and then she feels him relax under her.

"My brothers and I were born during the mid-sixteenth century in Salon-de-Provence, in the South of France. Our father was the astrological consultant to the Queen Consort of France. It was there he met our mother, Adrienne; she was a member of King Henry II's kitchen staff. When my mother met my father, Michel, he was already married to a non-Nephilim woman named Anne, had children with her. He loved his wife, but he fell in love with our mother, and she fell in love with him. She became his mistress, our father's sister; our aunt, Henri's mother, took her in. Our father Michel took her and our aunt under his protection, he was very protective of us all. Our father's mother, our grandmother had died when he was very young; his father became an alcoholic, and when he drank, he would become violent towards him and his sister, Henri's mother, our aunt. When I found this out about our father, I came to understand why he felt so protective of us. A combination of his past and knowing how valuable our family was. Our aunt possessed a rare ability, we were never told what that ability was, just that she had many people wanting her to work for them, and not for the power of good. The day after Markus's thirteenth birthday, our father died, leaving us vulnerable. His wife, jealous of his love for our mother, his love for us, and his over-protection for Henri, and our aunt, went to the King, telling him of what we were, and of our abilities. The morning after our father's death, the King's guards came to take us all. My mother and aunt once showed my brothers, Henri, and I, a secret passage that our father had built in preparation; he knew that day would eventually come. Not long after the invasion Athena, Apollo, and a young Nephilim guard member came to our rescue. When Athena found my brothers, Henri and I hiding in the secret passage, she instructed us to follow it and not to look back, that it would lead to a crypt in the cemetery. There, a member of the guard would be waiting for us." Atticus closes his eyes.

"I remember hearing the screams of my mother and my aunt, the shouting, the commotion of a battle happening behind us." Atticus opens his eyes and looks down at her.

"Walking through that secret passage felt like a walk of a thousand miles. When we reached the crypt, a young male Nephilim guard was waiting for us, just as Athena had said. He was wearing a rucksack and holding five more. He gave a rucksack to each of us and told us to change. I had wondered who the fifth backpack was for, now I know, it must have been for Pierre, I mean Alex. I remember when I opened the strange material bag that the guard member gave me, when I peered into it; I remember thinking what strange clothing. You see at the time; we were unaware that we were about to be taken to another time. The clothes in the rucksacks were the clothes that were being worn in the time we were going to be taken to. We did as the guard said, we changed into the clothing provided. After we had changed, the guard member burned our old clothes, shrugged off his own backpack. And then from the inside of his bag, he pulled out some water bottles, sandwiches, and some fruit. He handed us all a bottle of water, a sandwich, and an apple each, told us we needed to eat before the journey."

"Henri being the eldest asked him what journey, but he simply told us that Athena, and Apollo would explain. The rest is ancient history…so to speak." Atticus looks down at her again, she places her hand gently on his face.

"Thank you for telling me."

He smiles a warm, loving smile, moves her hair behind her ear and starts to lean his face towards hers. They slide into a position where Lola is on her back, his face hovering above hers. She pulls his face closer to hers, and just as they're about to kiss, both their communicators bleep. He lets out a completive moan, sits himself up, and then Lola does the same. He presses the answer call button, and Athena's face is projected.

*

When Atticus answers Athena's call, she did not expect him to be in bed with Lola, she tries to cover up her surprise of seeing them in bed together, by going straight to the point.

"Zeus has informed me of your predicament. Have you heard from Josiah?"

Atticus shakes his head.

"No, the Nazis must have taken his communicator from him."

"Zeus has located him. The Nazi base, where they are keeping him, is about a mile North of the inn. Apollo, Markus, Henri, Lachesis, Atropos, and I, we're trying to find out more about the soldiers posted there. As soon as we do, Lachesis, Atropos, and I will come to you. Atticus?"

"Yes?"

"We will try and get to you by tomorrow night, but you may want to book your rooms for another night, just in case." Atticus nods in understanding.

"We will try. It's busy here, we were lucky to have grabbed the last available room for tonight. What should we do if this room has already been reserved for tomorrow night? Is there another public house nearby?" Atticus asks her. Markus's face appears next to Athena's. When he sees Lola and Atticus in bed together, he chuckles, before continuing.

"There is another public house, farther down the road from your current one. Head south." Markus holds up the map and points to a second public house. Atticus nods. Markus's face disappears leaving Athena's face the only one in view.

"We will try your current location first. If you and Lola are not there, we will make our way to the second accommodation. If we are able to get to you by tomorrow night, we shall likely not arrive until late." Atticus nods in understanding. "Good night, Atticus, Lola. Do not worry about Josiah, Zeus is keeping an eye on him. So far, the Nazis have him locked up in a cell, but have not attempted to do him any harm, just asked him some questions. They cannot do anything further unless evidence appears against him, which will not happen. The Nephilim guard there are making sure of it."

"Night, Athena," says Atticus.

"Thank you, Athena," says Lola. Athena nods them farewell and ends the call. As Athena ends the call, Apollo enters her office.

"How are they?"

"Honestly? They looked cosy. I think I may have interrupted something." Apollo takes a seat on the sofa.

"Do you think they have discovered their past connection?" Apollo enquires.

"No. I do not think so. I think they both know they share a profound bond, but no, not about their past connection." Athena looks up from studying the map that is placed on the desk in front of her and looks at her brother considerately. "What about you?" Athena enquires.

"What about me?"

Athena gets up from the seat behind her desk and walks over to him.

"Now that he is older; he has grown into a man that thinks the way he does, he has developed uncanny character traits to those of his prior life as your son. Do you find it hard being around him, knowing that he is not him, but is so like him?"

Apollo considers his sister's question for a moment before answering. He turns to look at her.

"Sometimes. But then I remind myself that this is a different life, a different time, and that he is not my son. He is a man, living a different life; no two incarnation journeys are the same, they are not the same person. Also, what he is meant to learn during this life, is different to what he was meant to have learned in that life. Therefore, the outcome of this life will be different to the outcome of that life, and I trust that he

128

has evolved." Apollo stands, Athena follows. He places a comforting hand on his sister's arm.

"We always knew they would incarnate together again, eventually. I should leave you to continue your research, the sooner you get to them, the better."

*

Josiah's eyes are just starting to drift shut when he hears the popping teleportation sound. He opens his eyes and sits up, almost banging his head on the cold, damp stone that the camping bed is resting against.

Standing in the cell beside his bed, is Kevin. Josiah swings his legs off the bed, planting his feet firmly onto the hard stone floor.

"About time somebody showed! What's the plan?" Kevin hands Josiah a new communicator.

"Hide this! Athena and the Moirai sisters are on their way to meet Atticus and Lola." Kevin walks over to a large crack that's running up the wall opposite Josiah's bed and presses his hand firmly against it.

"When the red-light flashes on the communicator, place your hand here, and press." The grey stone beneath Kevin's hand shimmers, then disappears, revealing a stone staircase leading down into darkness. Shivers rocket up and down Josiah's spine as he walks over to peer down the steps into the darkness. Kevin continues,

"Hopefully, you will be out of here by tomorrow night. Atticus, and the Moirai sisters will be at the other end waiting for you. *Do not* attempt to escape until that red light flashes. There are Nazis standing on watch all around this place, you will be caught. Understand?" Josiah nods. They hear some heavy footsteps approaching, Kevin places his hand back on the area where the solid wall was before the area shimmered and vanished, the wall reappears. Kevin nods his head, and teleports out, leaving Josiah once more, alone. The Nazi soldiers do not come to collect Josiah, they walk past his cell. They stop at the cell next to his, he hears the prisoner begging them for mercy. Josiah goes and sits back onto the camp bed, as the soldiers drag the prisoner past his cell. The sight of his bloodied, swollen face, his bloodied body, makes Josiah wince and look away.

As he lies back down and closes his eyes; he can hear the tortured screams of the fellow prisoner in the distance. He places his hands over his ears to try and block out the screams of pain, he squeezes his eyes shut tighter. A flashback of when the King's men came to take them away—them rushing to hide in the place they hid before Henri rushed them into the secret passageway; the screams of his aunt and his mother as he, Henri, and his brothers fled their childhood home—enters his mind. Tears leak from his eyes, and start to roll down his cheeks, he wipes them away with his hand.

Chapter Nine

Lola opens her eyes to discover a lady with skin the colour of coffee, black hair in a long braid, wearing a plain grey dress leaning over her. Lola recognises her immediately from the photographs her father had showed her of the lady and her mother.

"Amita!" Lola sits up and embraces her, the lady pulls herself from Lola's embrace.

"Who is Amita? It's me, Leuce." *'I am dreaming.'* Lola realises. She looks around to see where she is; it's a place she has never dreamt of before. She is in a meadow; the grass has a dull green colour and there are little grey flowers everywhere. She looks up at the sky, it's filled with dark grey storm clouds, and lightning bolts that continuing to flash. She looks at the lady who looks likes her mums old friend Amita.

"Where am I?"

"You are in The Asphodel Meadows, in the underworld."

Lola glances around at her surroundings once more, this time she sees others, all wearing the same plain grey cotton clothing, all wandering around, doing nothing in particular, looking lost. She pulls herself up, and looks at Leuce.

"I don't belong here. I have to wake up."
The look on Leuce's face, Lola knew that look, it is the look of pity, she thinks Lola is in denial; she does not believe she is dreaming, but Lola knows that she is.

Lola glances down at herself, she is wearing the same grey cotton clothing that everyone else is wearing. She looks down at her hands; her hands were not her own. These hands are smaller than her own, the skin is olive and possesses a grey undertone, her own hands are bigger, and her skin, although olive, is lighter. This has never happened before—she has never dreamt whilst still possessing her current consciousness, physically being the woman in the dream, but thinking, and viewing things as if it her own present consciousness. Lola was not sure how this is possible; to overtake the consciousness of a prior life with her current consciousness. But somehow, she has, and she's not sure how to escape, how to return to her own body, how to wake up. She looks at Leuce.

"How did I get here?"

"I do not know. What is the last thing you remember?" Lola tries to recall where she was…before she was there. She was in bed lying next to Atticus, in Kielce in 1939, but she cannot tell Leuce that. So instead, she thinks back to prior dreams that she has had and lies.

"I was being chased through some woods."

Leuce wraps her hand around Lola's wrist.

"Follow me" But before they take their first step a man, tall, muscular, older man with dark olive skin, black hair and a matching beard that rests on his chest, appears before them, holding a bident. Next to him a Cerberus starts to growl at them.

"How did you get here? You do not belong here!" he shouts in anger as he points the bident towards Lola. She hears a high-pitched music note, and instantaneously is pulled back into her own body, back to 1939, back to her body that is lying in bed next to Atticus, she wakes with a gasp.

132

Atticus pulls her into his arms. Lola's heart is racing, and she is dripping in sweat. Atticus kisses the top of her head.

"It's okay, Lola, it was only a dream." He softly says. She feels her heartbeat start to slow down as she slowly becomes aware of her surroundings. She feels Atticus's warm breath, his warm body beside her. Someone starts to knock on their door. Atticus climbs out of bed and answers it, revealing a rugged, fair-haired boy, wearing a flat cap, around fifteen years old. He is holding a tray with some bread and butter, a knife, a jug of orange juice, a jug of water, a bar of soap and two small glasses, and two face cloths.

"Breakfast, sir, and some washcloths for you and your lady friend."

Atticus takes the tray and the cloths from the young boy.

"Thank you."

The boy tilts his cap.

"You're welcome, sir!" The boy walks off. Atticus places the tray onto the bed. Lola sits herself up and breaks off some of the bread and starts to butter it. Atticus's eyes are watching her, studying her like a hawk

"Do you often have nightmares that cause you to wake shouting?"

"I woke up shouting. What did I shout?"

"No. You woke shouting, 'No', but before that you were talking, you were dreaming of talking to someone named Leuce. Who is she?" Lola takes a bite of the bread and butter and shrugs.

"I don't know. You already know I sometimes dream about strangers."

"Yes, but you never told me that those dreams… were nightmares."

133

"That's because it's rare that they are nightmares. When they first started, when I didn't understand what they were, I was scared. But as I grew, I began to understand what they were and my fear of them went. Last night, was the first time in years that one became a nightmare. Maybe my abilities are strengthening, and it's a side effect. I'm sure it was a one off." She says reassuring him before climbing out of the bed.

She picks up one of the washcloths, and the jug of water and makes her way over to the single dusty mirror hanging on the wall and begins to wash her face. She glances at Atticus's face in the reflection, the cogs turning in his brain.

"You should eat something." He breaks off a piece of the bread, butters it and eats it. She thinks back to the dream; '*Maybe Athena will know how my consciousness was able to possess the body of past me.*'

*

"Nowak!" one of the Nazis shouts as he beams a flashlight onto Josiah's face.

"Visitor!" *A visitor? Lola, Atticus?* Josiah pulls himself up from the camp bed and squints towards the bright light shining on him. Outside his cell stood a lady in a navy woollen cloak, the hood of the cloak is hiding her face from his view.

"Lola!" Josiah runs over to the bars, at a closer look, he can tell the woman is not Lola. This woman is shorter, smaller in frame.

"Who are you?"
"A friend," her voice is soft. He can barely hear her.

"A friend? Have you come to get me out?" the woman, she shakes her head.

"No, I wanted to be sure it was you… Josiah." The mystery lady says his name in a soft whisper.

"Why won't you take down your hood? Show me your face? Do I know you?"

"Yes Josiah, you know me. I cannot reveal my identity to you yet, but I will in time. I had to make sure that it was you that I had seen. Is Atticus here with you in this time also?"

"Yes."

The stranger glances over her left shoulder at the soldier and pulls the cloak further forward.

"I have to go." Before Josiah has the chance to ask her any more questions, she leaves.

*

When Athena walks through the dolmen into 1939 Kevin is there waiting for her.

"I hope you have not been waiting long?" Athena asks him.

"Not at all. Only a few minutes," he answers. Athena is wearing a powder blue tea dress, a long woollen coat and a pair of black t-strap shoes. He holds out his arm for her to take and he teleports them both to a nearby field. Kevin offers his arm to her and offers to carry her suitcase. Athena gives him her suitcase.

"It has been a while, Kevin. You are looking well. How is Katherine?" Athena and Kevin share a romantic history and Athena often wondered what her life would have been like if she had said yes to his marriage proposal. She knows that the woman who had said yes to him, is now pregnant. She wonders if that would have been her, if she had stayed, instead of travelling back in time to rescue the Hardy boys. Athena had always wanted to get married and have children but every time an opportunity like that arose for her, she was called to go on a mission by her father.

She thinks about Lola. If she had accepted Kevin's proposal, she knew Lola would not have been born, she knew that Lola was the Nephilim they had had been waiting for. Along with the Hardy boys, they are the Nephilim that the prophecy had been made about the key to saving the Nephilim race.

"How is Josiah? How was he when you visited him?" she asks him.

"I went to check in on him before coming to meet you. Athena, just as I teleported in, the Nazi's were dragging him into the cell, they never saw me, but Athena, the Nazis have found something to use against him. He will be unable to walk, the Nazis had made the soles of his feet red raw. Blood was dripping from them." Athena stops in her tracks.

"What?" her voice is filled with fear. Kevin continues to update her.

"I was able to teleport into the office and read his report. They have found a problem within his documents; suspect they are fake"

Athena furrows her brows, but continues to walk towards the public house, speeding up her pace, until they reach the gate and stop.

"That will make his escape more complicated." Athena says anxiously. They start to walk down the footpath that leads to the public house where Atticus and Lola remain.

"Somebody will have to meet him in the cell to assist him. We will need a new plan, which means we need more time."

"Athena, I am not sure how much more he will be able to take." Kevin comments with concern.

"I understand, but it would be dangerous to go ahead with a rescue mission without taking his condition into consideration. He won't be able to walk, therefore he will need someone to assist him."

Kevin sees an idea pop into Athena's mind.

"Kevin, do you think you would be able to get one of the uniforms of one of the officers placed there?"

"Yes. I think so."

"I have an idea. When do you think you will be able to get one by?"

"I can get one tonight."

"Do you think you could get some of the soldier's blood also?" Kevin nods.

"No problem," he reassures her.

They approach the front entrance of the public house.

"Thank you. As soon as you have the items bring them to me."

Kevin gives Athena her suitcase back.

"What should I tell Josiah?" he asks her.

"Tell him that we have another plan, but we need another day. Tell him what he discovers must never be told to another. Tell him to keep faith, and that we are doing all we can to get him out of there as soon as we are able too, hopefully tomorrow, late evening."

Kevin says his goodbyes, Athena enters the bar. The public house is not as busy as it was when Atticus and Lola first entered. Athena makes her way to the bar where the older barman is crouched down behind the bar, cleaning.

"Excuse me?"

The man behind the counter finishes drying a glass.

"What would you like?" he asks her.

"I am meeting a couple here, they checked in last night. Pierre Nowak, and Marie Dudek?"

"One moment, Ma'am." The gentleman walks further down the bar, bends down, and pulls out a notebook. He walks back over to her and opens it.

"Room eleven. May I ask who is asking for them, who you are?"

"I am his aunt, Magdalena Nowak," Athena answers. The man nods.

"Follow me please," the round-bellied barman instructs. Athena picks up her suitcase and follows the man to their room, she knocks.

*

Josiah is laying on his side, curled up in the foetal position when he hears the familiar popping of someone who has just teleported in. Kevin walks over to him and crouches down beside him. He places a comforting hand on Josiah's arm. Josiah turns over to face him. Kevin places his hand softly onto Josiah's wrist, Josiah is in bad condition. His eyes have started to develop dark circles beneath them. His eyes are red, bloodshot, and puffy from where he knew Josiah had been crying and he is starting to look paler. Josiah quietly speaks.

"Is it time? It has not flashed red?"

Kevin shakes his head.

"No. Athena has had to come up with a new plan, since you won't be able to walk. They need some more time. It has been moved to tomorrow night."

138

"Can't you teleport me, us both out of here?"

"If I could, I would. The walls have some kind of lead in them which drains my abilities and strength considerably. I barely have enough strength to teleport myself in and out." *Silence.*

"Listen Josiah, Athena says the new plan will involve you finding out something, something that needs to be kept a secret. She has asked me to tell you that whatever you discover you must never tell to another, do you understand?" Josiah nods.

"Okay. I must go now, there is something I must do." Kevin leans over to Josiah's ear.

"Keep faith, we are doing all we can." Kevin stands back up

"Tomorrow night," he says before teleporting out.

*

Lola opens the door. When she sees Athena, she embraces her.

"You're here!"

Athena thanks the gentleman for showing her to their room and enters.

"Where is Atticus?"

Lola takes her case from her.

"He went for a walk."

"A walk? I thought I made it clear that exploring was not allowed, any kind of interaction could cause the timeline to change."

"He knows, he will not interact with anybody. He just needed to get some air. Where are the Moirai?"

Athena takes off her jacket and places it on the bed and

takes a seat. Lola takes a seat next to her.

"They had a few errands to run. They will be here later. Actually, it's quite fortunate that we are able to have a moment alone, we have had to change the original plan. Josiah is wounded."

"Is he okay?"

"Not particularly, but he is remaining strong." Athena takes Lola's hand in her own.

"Lola, I need you to use your shapeshifting ability. We need you to take on the appearance of one of the Nazi officers. Kevin is going to meet us later with a uniform and some of their blood for you to use."

"Athena, I haven't been able to control that ability."

"I believe in you, Lola; you can do it. Josiah has been informed that the escape will be taking place tomorrow night instead, allowing us an extra day to train."

"Has he been told what to expect?" Lola asks.

"No. But he has been told that what he discovers *must* be kept secret."

"So, what is the plan?"

Athena releases Lola's hands.

"You will take on the appearance of one of the officers, then once in his cell, there is a wall. Zeus has temporarily turned the wall into a doorway leading into an underground tunnel . To access it you must place your hand on the wall, only when the light on this communicator—Athena places a communicator disguised as a watch around Lola's wrist— turns red. Once the light has turned red, and you to have place your hand on the wall. The doorway will appear that leads to a staircase, which leads to the tunnel. Atticus, and Kevin will be waiting for you both on the other side. Lachesis, Atropos, and I will distract the other soldiers. Once you're both out, you are to come straight back here."

"I have also bought you this," Athena takes out a vial from her jacket pocket. The vial contains some blood.

"It is Panacea's. When you take on the appearance of a Nephilim, you also access their abilities. I brought it…just in case anything happened. Josiah has been wounded Lola; he may need some healing. I will occupy the others, you can shapeshift into Panacea and heal him. We need him to recover as speedily as he can." Lola takes the vial from Athena and slips it into her own suitcase.

"Any questions?" Athena asks her.

"When I place my hand onto the wall, how will it read my print if my hand is the same as the soldiers?"

"It will not be reading your print. It will be reading your energy. The ability to shapeshift only changes your appearance, your energy does not change."

"Where will I be changing?"

"There is an alley. Once Atticus, and Kevin are out of sight, you will change, and again before exiting the passage from the cell."

Atticus enters the room, before Lola and Athena can continue their conversation. When Atticus sees Athena, he rushes over to her and embraces her, the way a son would greet his mother after not seeing her for a while.

"You reached us before nightfall. How is Josiah? Where are Lachesis and Atropos?" he says noticing that Athena has come alone.

"They will be here later. Listen Atticus, the Nazis have flogged Josiah's feet. He is unable to walk without assistance, so we have had to come up with a new plan. The rescue

141

mission will have to happen tomorrow night instead."

"But Athena, we cannot allow him to be there any longer. We must help him now!"

"Atticus, if we were to go ahead tonight as planned, we will fail and we will all be caught. He cannot walk without assistance; we need to plan a distraction and break into his cell. If we do not, we will be putting ourselves at risk at being caught by the Nazis also. Please try to understand."

Atticus takes off his jacket and seats himself next to Athena.

"Tell me what you need me to do."

*

The sun is setting in the sky when Kevin reaches the Nazis' station. He has placed himself at the corner of the building, where he has a clear view of the front of the station. Peering around the edge of the wall, he keeps his eyes on the door that leads to the inside of the station. He is carrying a satchel, wearing a wide brim black hat, a pair of black leather gloves, and a long black trench coat to match. He has wrapped a dark brown scarf around his neck, mouth, and nose, to help cover the majority of his face, concealing his identity.

After an hour of waiting, a lone Nazi finally exits the building. Kevin takes out a handkerchief that he has covered in Chloroform from his jacket pocket and teleports to behind the officer, covers the officer's nose and mouth with the handkerchief, knocking the officer unconscious instantly.

Kevin teleports them both to a remote location in the middle of a forest. He strips the soldier of his clothes, leaving him in his undergarments. He pulls out a needle and a small glass vial that has a plastic lid, from his coat pocket. Using his mouth, he unscrews the lid, and with the needle pricks the Nazi soldier's index finger. He squeezes the Nazi's finger so droplets of his blood drip into the vial. When he's done, he screws the lid back on and places the vial back into his pocket. From his satchel he takes out multiple ropes, first he ties the soldier's wrists individually to the tree, then the soldier's ankles, leaving him tied to the tree in a starfish position. After completing the tying up, he teleports himself to the field that he and Athena were in earlier that day, leaving the Nazi unconscious, bound to the tree in the middle of nowhere.

*

When Kevin arrives back at the public house where Atticus, Lola, and Athena is staying; they are all sat around a table, with them are Lachesis and Atropos. Drinks and plates of food are on the table. Kevin takes a chair from another table to join them, seating himself next to Athena.

Kevin takes off the satchel and sneakily passes it to Athena under the table. Athena softly squeezes his hand in appreciation. Lola notices the tension between Athena and Kevin. She turns to Atticus, places a hand on his leg. He leans his head down to hear what she has to say.

"Have Kevin and Athena had a disagreement?" she asks him.

Atticus glances at them both. Apollo once told him that Athena was almost engaged to a man in the 1930s, looking at Athena and Kevin together now; Lola is right, something is going on between them. He wonders if Kevin is the man Apollo once referred too.

143

"It's possible, I'm sure."

"Now that we are all here…" Athena gains the attention of all that are sat around the table; she pulls out a hand drawn map of the Nazi station and the surrounding area.

"It is time to discuss the plan with everyone, make sure we are all on the same page, ensure that we all know our roles during the mission. It is a fairly straightforward plan. Josiah's cell is here," Athena points to a square drawn within the Nazi station.

"Zeus has temporarily created a passage leading from the cell to here," Athena points to an 'X' which is placed on a section of the map marked 'field'. "The exit into the field from the cell is a mile long." Lola raises her hand.

"Yes, Lola?"

"A mile long? You said Josiah's feet have been wounded. I am not strong enough alone to help Josiah through a mile long passage…" Athena looks at Kevin, as if Kevin had read her mind.

"Once I know Athena and the Moirai are safe, I will start to make my way through the tunnel, meeting you halfway." Lola nods in thanks.

"I don't understand why Lola has to be the one to break into his cell, and not me," says Atticus.

"Surely it would be safer, more logical if I were the one assigned that?"

"Zeus has programmed Lola's energy. I expect he has his own reasons as to why that role has been assigned to Lola," Athena comments.

"Maybe you should ask him if that is wise?" Atticus insists. Lola places her hand over his.

"It's okay Atticus, with Kevin's help I can do it." Lola

knows why Atticus doesn't want that to be her role; he wants to protect her, keep her safe and feels that the role may be putting her in a position of even more danger. Athena continues to talk through the plan.

"Lachesis, Atropos, and I will cause a distraction by saying we were attacked by a group of Jews. I hate to say such a thing, but it is Nazi soldiers that we will be distracting, so needs must. It will be a lie of course. Once we have their attention Lola will sneak into the station, pick the lock of Josiah's cell, and open the entrance into the tunnel, where Kevin will meet them halfway to help carry Josiah, the rest of the way."

"Atticus, I need you to stay guard of the exit. If anyone comes, you can use the concealment spell to hide yourself, and the passage. Atticus, your spell casting ability is one of the reasons why we thought you the best for the role of guard watch duty." Atticus glances at Lola, she squeezes his hand. He nods at Athena in understanding.

"Does everybody understand their role?" Athena asks looking around at the group. Kevin, Atticus, Lola, Lachesis, and Atropos nod in understanding.

"Good." Athena looks at her watch.

"Before it gets too late, Lola and I need to train." Athena stands up.

"Train?" Atticus says questioning.

"Yes. There are a few things that Lola and I need to work on, in preparation for tomorrow."

"Can I join?" he asks her.

"Not tonight. But tomorrow she will need to train some more in self-defence techniques, for which we will require your assistance. Lola?" Lola stands, she and Athena say

145

goodnight to the group and depart, leaving the rest of the group to continue with their evening.

Lola follows Athena to her room. The room is basic like the one Atticus, and she had shared the previous night, and again tonight as they were informed that a room had become free, but then 'her partner's aunt' had checked in.

Once they enter the room, Athena takes out an envelope and a Nazi soldier's uniform from the satchel Kevin had given to her. Athena instructs Lola that she needs to change into the uniform. The soldier's uniform drowned Lola, he is clearly a tall, well-built man, larger than any of the Hardy men. This surprised Lola, as the Hardy men are quite tall, and broad. When Lola finishes changing, Athena hands her the envelope; inside the envelope is a vial of blood.

Lola hands the empty envelope back to Athena. Athena presents Lola with a sewing needle. Lola pricks her own finger and dips her finger into the vial, touching some of the Nazi soldier's blood that Kevin had collected for her.

"Remember what I taught you in previous lessons. Close your eyes, imagine a warm ray of golden sunlight spreading through you, starting in the middle of your chest, slowly spreading down into your stomach, into your hips, down your legs, into your ankles, into your feet and coming out of your toes and into the ground. Spreading from your chest into your shoulders, down your arms, beaming out of your fingertips. Spreading up into your head and out of your crown chakra, the golden beams then connecting all around you. Imagine you are him, imagine you are him, imagine you are the Nazi soldier."

Lola feels the familiar wave of warmth sweeping through her, of her body changing, the familiar pull in her chest, as if she were being tugged and pulled in different directions. The feeling only lasts a few seconds, she knows she has changed but as usual, the change does not stick. That was her problem, she could change, no problem, but she's unable to make the changes stick. She opens her eyes and looks at Athena, exhaling a deep sigh of frustration.

"Again," Athena instructs, Lola repeats the previous process. Again, it does not stick.

"Why can't I make it stick?" Lola exasperates.

"Our abilities are linked to our emotions. If we are stressed, worried, angry, anxious, fearful, or are experiencing any contrasting emotions, they can prevent our abilities from working to their full potential. Lola, is there something on your mind?"

Lola thinks back to the dream she had the previous night, the dream she had when child Atticus visited her, and about her uncertainty about Atticus's feelings towards her.

"Lola?" Athena seats herself on the bed, pats the space next to her, instructing Lola to sit. Lola seats herself down.

"Lola, what is it? What is going on?"

Lola looks at her hands that are resting in her lap.

"You know you can trust me. You can talk to me about anything, even if you think that something seems trivial."

Lola looks at Athena, her face filled with concern.

"Lola, we need your appearance of the soldier to stick, for our plan to rescue Josiah to succeed. What is it that is playing on your mind?" Athena asks her again.

Lola looks back at her hands resting in her lap.

"There is something I wish to discuss with you; I would

147

like to talk to you about some dreams I have had."

"Okay."

Lola begins to tell Athena about them.

"I had a dream about Atticus. On the train journey here, a 'child him' came to me. He told me that he didn't have long to tell me what he needed to tell me. He said he saw me being born, saw me as a child, saw our son and daughter, and then he said he was born. He vanished before my eyes, before he finished telling me something else. I didn't understand it. Atticus was born hundreds of years before me, surely what I dreamt of cannot mean something, it was likely just a dream. But then I remembered when Atticus, Josiah and I were talking about their childhood. Atticus told me about when their mother would read to them, when they were in bed, before they went to sleep. What he had described, what they used to wear to bed, it was what the child Atticus was wearing in my dream."

"There is a belief that we choose what happens to us before we are born, that everything is pre-planned, one of the theories of what causes déjà vu. You feel as if you have experienced something before; because that was a moment that was pre-agreed."

"I don't understand."

Athena tries to explain the theory a little clearer.

"There are infinity timelines. Some Nephilim are rumoured to be able to travel through the different timelines. I am sure what you experienced was just a dream, in fact, I am positive. However, it is possible for someone's subconscious to travel through the different timelines. But Atticus does not possess that ability. So, the chance of that being the reason behind the dream is miniscule. It more than likely was just a dream. Is that all?"

148

"No. Another thing that has been playing on my mind is Atticus. I have always been spot-on when it comes to reading people, and Atticus and I seem to be stuck in a circle. His actions do not match his energy."

"What do you mean?" Athena asks, confused.

"Well, the energy I feel coming from him, is that he cares about me, profoundly. I know he feels protective of me. When we are in each other's presence the energy between us is magnetic. I sometimes catch him staring at me, I see him being affectionate towards other people, for example at my party; he allowed some of the women to drape themselves all over him, and he reciprocated just as affectionately back. But with me; he stopped hugging me in front of people after a month of us meeting. He sometimes even ignores me in front of others. He's choosing to not be open affectionately with me as he is with others, but then his energy tells me another story. It frustrates me, that his actions do not match his energy. When they don't match it makes me to want to ignore him back, which he the picks up on, and then he feels there is something wrong, which frustrates him. Then we both end up being frustrated with each other. I don't understand why he's perfectly okay being open with other women physically, but not with me; unless we're alone, he closes himself off completely."

"Lola, what you have to understand about Atticus is that Atticus, ever since he was a child, has been an affectionate individual, until it came to someone who he cares about deeply. It sounds like that when you first met, he was able to be open with you affectionately, like he is with everybody else, because he felt he was in no danger. Then as you grew to know each other better, your bond with each other grew deeper, his feelings towards you started to evolve. When he realised this, he closed himself off." Athena reflects on her words for a moment and continues to reassure Lola.

"Atticus, although he does not show it, is somewhat of a sensitive soul and when he falls for someone, he falls hard. The reason why his actions do not match his energy is likely due to him protecting himself. Lola, you, and Atticus share a profound bond and even though he is not affectionately open with you as he is with other individuals, anyone who sees you both together can see, can feel the bond you both have."

"So, what should I do? How can I prevent myself from getting frustrated when his actions and energy don't match?"

"Breathe. Try not think about his actions. Focus on the feeling of the love that you feel for each other. You do not need to take any action. Allow that love to flow through you; breathe and start doing something that brings you joy."

"Thank you, Athena. That has actually helped."

"I am glad. Was there anything else?"

"Yes. Last night I had a dream that I was in the past, and I was in a body I have dreamt about before; a 'past-life' body. But this time I wasn't just in the body. It's hard to explain, but it was like *I,* who I am today, my present consciousness was in that body too. I had my current mind, and although I did not look like how I physically do now. It felt like I was living my current life but, in my past-life's body. There was a woman there who looked like my mum's friend Amita, but when I called her Amita, she said that wasn't her name. She said her name was Leuce, and then this giant man appeared with a three-headed dog in front us and said, well shouted in anger that I did not belong there. Then I heard a high-pitched music note, and I was pulled back to now; that's when I woke up. Do you think I travelled, subconsciously?"

"Leuce was the name of a nymph that Hades fell in love with. He abducted her and took her to the Asphodel Meadows and trapped her there. She never escaped. It sounds like you may be developing the ability of Ergokinesis, the ability to manipulate energy forms." Athena takes out the map, turns it over to the blank side, then takes out a pen, draws a circle, then writes past, present, future in different places around the circle.

"Time has no start, no end. Everything as you already know, is made up of energy, including timelines. The past, the present, and the future are happening simultaneously. You have probably heard of people having premonitions, what premonitions are, are glimpses of a future that has already happened, in one of these existing timelines. As I mentioned earlier, sometimes our subconscious can travel to these other timelines, dimensions when we are asleep, or meditating. In a moment our individual frequency can change to match the frequency of that timeline, or dimension. If you are able to manipulate energy, you can manipulate your frequency, and if you are able to change your frequency to match a certain timeline or dimension frequency, then your subconscious mind, theoretically, should be able to take over the consciousness of who you are in that timeline, in that dimension. Does that make sense?"

"I think so. You are saying that my frequency changed to match the frequency of me from that time, and because it was a match, my subconscious was able to travel into that timelines body, taking over that consciousness."

"Exactly!"

"So, the musical note I heard?"

"Music can fine-tune frequencies. I think what happened

was that the musical note you heard, changed your frequency back to your current frequency, therefore pulling you back into your present body."

"But where did the musical note come from?"

"That I do not know. Maybe Hades produced it; knowing that you did not belong there, maybe he knows which musical note induces which frequency. I am not sure."

"Do you think that is how child Atticus was able to travel forward and appear in my dream?"

"I think the dream about child Atticus was just a dream." Athena says more than enthusiastically.

"Do you think those kind of dreams could happen again?" Lola feels Athena close herself off.

"It is unlikely." Athena is withholding information. Lola can feel that she is.

"Is that all?" Athena asks. Lola nods.

"Good. Shall we try again?"

Chapter Ten

The tallest of the Nazi soldiers that first interrogated Josiah, bends down and picks up the food tray that was left for Josiah at the door of his cell. The soldier looks down at the uneaten food, exhales and taking the tray with him, leaves. Minutes later he returns bringing a shorter soldier with him. The shorter soldier opens the cell door, they enter the cell and each grab an arm of Josiah's and drag him from his cell.

"It is disrespectful to us, to not eat the food we give to you." The taller of the two soldiers tell him, continuing to drag him down one of the corridors and into an empty room. When Josiah sees where they have dragged him to, he starts to fight against them. He wishes he were stronger, that he were able to use his abilities, but the combination of the lead in the walls, and the torture he has endured have left him defenceless.

"No! No you cannot do this to me again!" he screams at them. Two more soldiers come running into the room to assist. He's in the room the original two Nazi soldiers that had arrested him, made him look through the window into, the room they tortured the other prisoner in. It was also the same room in which they had previously tortured him too.

"We warned you that if you do not play nice, you will be punished. You disrespect and reject our kindness in feeding you, so now you pay. Strap him down!" the taller soldier instructs the other two officers that joined them in the room.

The two soldiers take Josiah from the taller and shorter Nazi's and force him to lay on his front, face down onto the table. They strap his wrists and ankles down to the frame of the table. The soles of Josiah's feet are facing upwards towards the ceiling. The shorter of the two soldiers that had dragged him into the room gives the taller one a bullwhip. The taller one walks to the foot end of the table and whilst tracing the soles of Josiah's feet with the whip he says,

"Maybe this will teach you some manners!"

The feel of the bullwhip tracing the soles of his feet cause Josiah to flinch. He hears the whooshing sound of the whip making its way through the air and closes his eyes in preparation for what he knew was about to happen, *crack... crack.* The pain is excruciating. Josiah closes his eyes tighter, picturing Lola's face; '*maybe if I imagine her face, the pain won't hurt as much.*'

*

Lola and Athena are in the pub garden.

"I hope you ladies have not been waiting long?" Kevin asks as he joins them in the garden.

"Where is everybody else?" he asks Athena. Athena looks at Lola and then back at Kevin.

"Actually, it's just you that Lola and I need to talk to." Athena looks at Lola and nods. Lola closes her eyes, feeling the warmth of her shapeshifting ability sweep over her, taking over. Once the change is complete, she opens her eyes and looks at Kevin.

"You're a shapeshifter." He doesn't seem surprised; he speaks the words as if possessing the shapeshifting ability is

154

the norm; '*Maybe he is also a shapeshifter.*' Lola closes her eyes and shift back into herself.

"I am guessing Lola's shapeshifting ability is going to play a big part in the rescue mission." Silence.

"I see, that is why you needed the Nazi uniform and the blood?" he asks addressing Athena.

"Yes."

"I should have guessed." Kevin walks over to one of the wooden benches and takes a seat.

"It is a dangerous plan, Athena. I don't like it. What if another Nephilim sees her change, a Nephilim who has allied themselves with the S.G.E.?" Kevin and Athena are talking amongst themselves ignoring the presence of Lola. Lola interferes, attempting to reassure him.

"We have a plan. A good one."

"What is the plan?" he asks Athena, dismissing Lola's interference.

"We will keep the uniform in the satchel. If anybody asks what's inside the satchel, we will simply tell them first aid products. Considering the mission, and Josiah's condition, I doubt anyone will question it. Lola will remain in her normal clothes until you have teleported Atticus to the field, and until Lachesis, and Atropos have left us to cause the commotion in front of the station. Once Lola and I are alone, Lola will change. Once you are clear from the Nazis you will teleport back to me, collect the satchel containing her clothes before teleporting to the field to open the exit from the tunnel with Atticus. Once the exit has been opened, as planned, you will meet Lola and Josiah inside, before you all exit to meet Atticus; Lola will change back into her original clothes. If Lola needs to do any healing to help Josiah; once clear of the Nazi prison Lola will stop and heal as needed, and then cover his feet in bandages. With his feet covered, no one will be able to see the healing Lola has done." Athena finishes telling Kevin.

"I have to admit, it does appear a well thought through plan,"

"What if the commotion doesn't engage the Nazi's interest?"

"Then Lachesis, and Atropos will go inside the station and distract them from the inside." Athena confidently says.

"Do the others know about your ability?" Kevin asks Lola.

"No. Just you. And Josiah will of course know after the mission, but we can trust him."

"Good. The less people know the better. I am guessing Athena has already spoken to you about the danger having this ability puts you and your loved ones in?"

"Yes."

"And you are able to control it?" he asks Lola with a fatherly affection. She glances at Athena.

"Lola is competent enough in her ability." Athena reassures him.

"Okay then," he comments, accepting Athena's plan.

*

Atticus is already in the middle of getting ready for the mission when Lola knocks on his door. When Athena arrived, booking the new empty double room, she thought it wise that Lola transfer and share with her rather than continue to share with Atticus. However, Lola had not had the chance to collect her case from Atticus' room until now.

156

"Lola! Come in," he says inviting her in. She walks over to her case, picks it up and turns to face him but places her case back down onto the floor.

"I need to tell you something. But I don't know how to."

"Okay," he says with uncertainty.

"I had a dream about you." she admits to him awkwardly.

"Was it a bad dream?" he asks cautiously.

"No. I dreamt of you as a child."

"Me as a child?" he asks confused. Lola seats herself onto his bed, he sits down next to her.

"We were at a garden party. I think it might have been a wedding reception; all the women were wearing evening dresses and all the men were wearing suits, or shirts and trousers. You went to get us both drinks from the bar, the bar was in the garden. I was standing at the top of some stone steps. I saw a little boy running through the crowd, towards me wearing the long white night shirt. When the boy grew closer to me, it was you. You were around five or six years old. You were panting from the running, you told me that you needed to tell me something, but you didn't have much time. You told me that you saw me being born, saw me as a child and then you were born." *It's probably best that I don't tell him everything that he said or happened in the dream.* "You were going to tell me something else but then you vanished before you could."

"I vanished?"

"Yes. I think the time limit you mentioned had run out. After you vanished, I looked over at 'present you', you knew I had seen something. You took me into some kind of greenhouse and then…"

"And then?"

157

"And then I woke up."

"Why were you worried about telling me about that?"

"I was worried, because I didn't want you to think I was crazy."

"Lola, no matter what you tell me, nothing would ever make me see you any differently. I already know and accept that you sometimes have dreams that are not normal dreams. I accepted that part of you a long time ago and look I am still here."

It's true what he says. In the past when Lola has confided in him; something that when she might have told others previously, they had decided to abandon their friendship, he has not. If anything, it has made their connection stronger. She knew that her doubt in telling him, was her own insecurity. He has proven to her time and time again, that no matter what happens she would, could never lose him and his friendship.

Lola thinks back to one conversation they had when the actual words Atticus used were *'I wish you would stop worrying about losing me. Even when you push me away. I am not going anywhere, no matter what you tell me, or what you do. I am not going to go anywhere.'* Lola takes a deep breath and exhales.

"I spoke to Athena about it, she thinks it was just a dream."

"I think she's right. I mean I think I would remember dreaming about travelling into the future and seeing you," he says reassuringly.

"You're probably right," she says returning the reassuring smile.

"Are you ready for tonight?" he says changing the subject.

"I am. Are you?"

"More than ready to get Josiah out of there. I'm just worried," he says.

"Worried?"

"Yes. I'm worried about how his time in there may have affected him. We Hardy boys have already been through our fair share of trauma. I'm scared the Josiah we rescue tonight will not be the Josiah we know." It touches Lola how much Atticus loves and cares for his brother.

"That is something I have been thinking about too. But Josiah is strong, he has lots of people who love and care about him, who will support him. It may take a while for him to heal fully psychologically but having those people around him in his life will help. Can I ask you something? Something about what happened?"

"Anything." Atticus responds.

"Why did Henri go with Apollo, instead of going with you and your brothers, and Athena?"

"Actually, Markus also went with Apollo at first. Apollo thought it would be safer to separate us. Just in case any of the S.G.E. were amongst the King's men and decided to follow us into the future. He thought they would likely look for three brothers if they had, so we were separated. Markus didn't come and stay with Athena permanently until he had turned eighteen, until the majority of his abilities had developed, and he had joined the guard."

"Majority of his abilities? I thought our abilities stopped developing once we have turned eighteen?"

"For women, yes. But the male Nephilim continue to develop until we're twenty-one."

"So, Markus and Henri, they now have all of their abilities. But you and Josiah, yours are still developing?" she asks curiously.

"Yes,"

"And mine, the abilities I have developed, they are the abilities I will now always have? No more?"

"That is correct, although you might. I mean you are eighteen for another six months, you may develop more between now and your nineteenth birthday. Hasn't your dad, or Athena, had the Nephilim puberty talk with you?"

"Nephilim puberty talk?"

"Yes. The talk about when our abilities start to kick in or stop developing?"

"No, they haven't," she informs him awkwardly.

"Oh Lola, Lola," he says, tutting. "Would you like me to give you the talk?" he asks teasingly.

"Well, you've already informed me that the female Nephilim abilities stop developing when they're eighteen and the male Nephilim stop at twenty-one."

"Yes. Would you like to know when they start to develop?" Atticus continues to inform Lola of the 'Nephilim puberty' process.

"First off, we are all born with our abilities, it's just they remain dormant until general puberty kicks in. However, sometimes Nephilim can 'accidentally' access their abilities before then. I remember once I made my mother and father so mad because I accidentally froze our pet cat Terrance. I mean they didn't stay mad at me for long, they couldn't, because they knew I had no idea how, or what I had done. It was after that incident that they sat Markus, Josiah, Henri, and I down and gave us the talk."

"You froze your cat?"

"Yes. Then during my thirteenth year, my ability of

Thermokinesis started to fully kick in."

"How many abilities does a Nephilim usually develop?"

"It's different for everyone. Some Nephilim only develop one, others I have heard about have developed up to five. I guess it depends on our parents; it's logical that a Nephilim born from two Nephilim parents would likely develop more abilities than a Nephilim born to one Nephilim parent."

"And how many do you have?"

"So far; three. The first one I developed was Thermokinesis. Then I discovered I was also a spell caster, and more recently Telumkinesis. Although I must ask you; please do not mention to anyone about the last one. It is very recent, and I'm not sure yet how it works."

"Who would I tell? Do you think you will develop any more?"

"Maybe, since I won't be entering my twenty-first year for another eighteen months. What about you?"

"What about me?"

"Apart from your aqua and earth manipulation, have you developed any additions?"

"Athena thinks because I was able to travel to a past life me and take over that body's conscious, I may have the ability of Ergokinesis; the ability to manipulate energy. She thinks I was able to manipulate my own energy, changing my frequency to match the frequency of a past-life' me, therefore enabling my subconscious, or conscious to take over that life's conscious."

Atticus draws his eyebrows into a frown.

"You never told me about that."

"It was the dream I had last night when I was with you."

"You never told me what you had dreamt about." he says

to her, annoyance in his tone.

"It wasn't a big deal. I didn't think it was something worth mentioning."

"Lola, travelling to a past life, and taking over that past life consciousness *is* a big deal! What if you were unable to travel back? What if you became trapped there? What would happen to present you? Your consciousness? Your body?" He stands up sharply and starts to pace back and forth. He stops pacing and turns to face her.

"Would you have died?"

"I don't know. Look, Athena thinks it's nothing to worry about." she says attempting to reassure him.

"Lola, Athena doesn't know everything!" he says, clearly angry with her.

"Why are you angry with me?" she asks him confused.

"You should have told me about this. Your subconscious physically leaving your body is something you should have told me about." He replies anxiously.

"You've dreamt of past lives too before."

"Yes. But that's only re-living subconscious memories, not actually travelling back to that life."

"I'm sorry." He starts to calm down, and seats himself back down onto the bed. Lola takes a seat next to him.

"What happened? Where did you go?"

"I was in the Asphodel Meadows."

"The Asphodel Meadows? Aren't they located in the underworld?" Before Lola has a chance to answer his question, someone knocks on the door.

"This conversation isn't over," he tells her before getting up and answering the door, revealing Kevin.

"It's time." Kevin informs them, they follow him to the pub's garden where Athena, Lachesis, and Atropos are waiting. Athena has the satchel containing the Nazi uniform hung over her shoulder.

"Is everyone clear in what they are doing?" everyone nods.

"Atticus. You're up first." Atticus takes hold of Kevin's arm, he teleports out. Minutes later Kevin teleports back, Lachesis and Atropos are the next to go.

"Lola. Are you sure you are ready?" Athena asks affectionately.

"I know how to make it stick. I just hope we don't run into any complications." Athena places her hand on Lola's shoulder in a motherly gesture.

"We won't," she says reasserting her confidence in the plan.

Kevin teleports back, they each take hold of an arm of his. They feel the strange sucking sensation take hold as they are sucked into the time and space force.

Chapter Eleven

"We might be in luck." Athena says as she peers around the wall looking at the deserted street where the prison is located.

"Maybe everyone is too scared to hang around here?" Lola says.

"Possibly," Lachesis says.

"Ready?" Athena asks them.

Lachesis, Atropos, and Kevin head to the front of the building and start to act rowdy, yelling and shouting. Two Nazi soldiers exit the building to see what's causing the commotion. Kevin makes his exit and starts to run, as predicted, one of the soldiers takes to chase him, whilst the other soldier takes Lachesis and Atropos into the station. Lola changes into the Nazi uniform, shapeshifts and then follows them into the station. When Lola enters, the soldier talking to Lachesis and Atropos nod at her in acknowledgement. She approaches the reception desk.

"Is everything okay?" She asks the soldier.

"Yes, sir. These young ladies have just been attacked, by a Jew." he comments.

"I see. Have you taken the report?" *Isn't that the kind of thing that they usually say in movies?*

"Just about to sir," he replies.

"The office may be better suited to do that than here, wouldn't you agree?" Lola advises. The soldier nods and instructs Lachesis and Atropos to follow him.

Now with two of the soldiers preoccupied, the station is sparse. The keys are easier to find than Lola expected, they are in the first drawer she opens. This station must have been one of the smallest, as there aren't many keys to choose from. Lola thinks back to the map of the station that was shown to her; according to the map the stairwell that leads down into the cells is located through the double doors, then the last door on the left.

She walks through the doors, and down the corridor at a steady, calm, confident pace; '*I have to look as if I belong.*' The corridor walls are painted white, the doors leading to the various rooms are wooden. She passes through the door leading to the stairwell that lead down to the prison cells. One of the officers is walking up the stairs towards her, he stops in front of her and raises his hand to give her the sieg heil salute.

"Heil Hitler!" She copies him, he continues to walk past her. As Lola continues to make her way down the stairwell, the further down she stepped the colder it became.

The stairwell ends in front of a large wooden door. The door has two large brass door bolts attached to it, she examines the keys in her hand, and the locks; they all look the same. She starts to try each key, the fifth and sixth ones unlock the bolts, she slides the bolts and pulls open the door. The basement, where the prison cells had been built, is beyond freezing. The walls and the ceiling containing them appear to be stone. Lola can see the damp glisten on them as light from the stairwell she has just entered from, gleams onto them. The smell makes her heave, it smells like mould, rot, urine, and dirt all mixed in together. '*How could they keep people in these conditions?*' The clarity of the neglect, and the conditions, fill her with rage.

She starts to check each cell looking for Josiah; she finds him in the third cell.

"Josiah?" The sight of him lying on his side, neglected, feet bloody, brings twisted knots to the pit of her stomach.

"Josiah?" she says again; he turns over to face her and starts to scream,

'No!' he is petrified.

"Josiah, it's me, it's Lola!" she says in attempt to calm him.

"No, no! You're lying!" he screams. Lola finds the correct key, and rushes over to him and kneels down beside him.

"Josiah, you have to be quiet, or we will be caught." The communicator on his wrist starts to flash red. He looks at her, his eyes filled with fear, it sends shivers up and down her spine. The Josiah that she had known, that Josiah was vibrant and full of life, that Josiah was not present.

His eyes are full of fear, frozen on her face. She holds up the communicator wrapped around her wrist that is also flashing red and shows him.

"See? You can trust me. I have come to get you out." Lola places his arm around her neck to help him stand.

"Lean on me."

He starts to pull himself up, following her instruction; but as soon as he places a foot down to walk, he collapses. Lola catches him before he falls.

"I can't," he says, his voice filled with defeat. Lola kneels down onto the floor to examine the soles of his feet; they have open slashes all over them; 'Think Lola.' she look at the door to the cell, and listens, she hears nothing, they're okay; 'Panacea, I can change into Panacea and use her healing abilities, to ease the soreness.'

166

"Okay. Josiah, I am going to change." Lola closes her eyes and pictures Panacea, what it was like to be her before, during her training. A small gasp escapes Josiah, she opens her eyes. Josiah is looking at her, his jaw slightly lowered in awe. Lola places her palms facing the soles of his feet, imagining a ray of white light shining down onto her, flowing into the top of her head, through her body and around her like Athena had instructed.

Josiah lets out a sigh of relief. The healing energy flowing from her palms is doing what she had hoped. She watches the shade of bright pink from the soreness starts to dull into a calmer shade of pink, helping to ease the pain of his wounds. She looks up at him, a spark of life has ignited back into his eyes.

"We have a lot to talk about." Lola claps her hands together stopping the stream of healing energy flowing from her palms into the soles of his feet.

She places his arm around her neck again to help him stand. Lola exhales a sigh of relief as he is able to place some pressure onto the soles of his feet.

They walk over to the wall, place our hands upon it, the area shimmers and fades away to reveal the steps leading down into darkness. Lola digs into one of the pockets of the Nazi uniform that is drowning her, in her physical appearance of Panacea...

*

"Thank goodness! You made it," Atticus says to Kevin.

"Of course, you doubted that I would?"

They kneel on the grass, and hold their palms down facing

the ground, the earth shimmers, a slope appears leading underground. They stand back up, Kevin salutes to Atticus before stepping onto the slope carrying the satchel containing the bandages and Lola's clothes.

*

The light from the flashlight illuminates the stairs before them. They pass through onto the top of the steps leading down. Lola turns around and places her palm on the area behind them where the wall used to be. The touch of her hands causes the area to glimmer once more, and the wall reappears behind them. The steps are slippery from the damp.

"Careful," Lola softly says to Josiah as they make their way down them. When they reach the bottom of the stairs, Lola takes Josiah's arm from around her neck and assists him in leaning against the cold stone wall. She closes her eyes and changes back into herself, before the change finishes Josiah throws his arms around her, embracing her, pulling her face to his and kisses her. A whooshing feeling sweeps up from the pit of her stomach and into her chest. She can taste the saltiness of tears and sweat upon his lips. His lips upon hers didn't feel as she had imagined,, a burning passion ignited within her, spreading like wild fire wanting more. He lets go and pulls himself away from her, leaving her frozen to the spot.

"Sorry. I shouldn't have…" Lola's interrupt him before he finishes his sentence.

"It's okay." A moment of silence creeps in.

"We have to keep going." Lola takes a step closer to him, he takes a step back.

"It's okay, Josiah. Come on, Kevin is expecting us." He

looks at her with uncertainty. She slowly takes another step towards him, narrowing the space between them. She lifts up his arm slowly placing it slowly back around her neck. He's embarrassed about kissing her.

"Not far to go now," She informs him.

"I can try to walk without your support?" Lola glances up at him, thinking back to the wounds she had seen.

"No. It's okay. I'm okay. I can do it." They hear the sound of footsteps approaching them coming from up ahead. "Kevin?" Lola shouts.

"Lola?" they hear him call back to them, his voice echoing, bouncing of the sides of the tunnel.

"Yes. It's us!" Lola shouts back, his fast-paced steps turn into running. When he sees them, he drops the satchel carrying her clothes and swoops in, taking Josiah from her.

Lola picks up the satchel and thanks him, and hands Kevin the bandages. Kevin and Josiah turn to face away from her as Lola changes back into her regular clothes, Kevin wraps Josiah's feet in the bandages. If Atticus, Lachesis, and Atropos saw Lola in the uniform they would discover what she was, and for now they cannot know, no one can.

"Ready." Lola says looping the strap of the satchel around herself. Kevin sweeps Josiah back into his arms effortlessly, as if Josiah weighed nothing at all, 'super strength perhaps?'

"Were you seen?" Kevin asks.

"No. I don't think so. What happened after the Nazis started to chase you?"

"When I was out of sight I teleported," he answers.

"What about Lachesis, Atropos, and Athena?"

"Safe. Back at the pub," he reassures her.

Kevin carrying Josiah, exits the tunnel before her; when

Atticus sees them, he rushes over to Kevin to assist him in supporting Josiah. Atticus flings himself around Josiah and rejoices. Taking Josiah's face into his hands, he kisses his forehead and says,

"You're okay. You're okay," before embracing him again.

"I need to get Josiah to Athena." Kevin says interrupting. Atticus still rejoicing at being reunited with his brother releases him from his grip.

"Of course! Of course!"

Kevin smiles, places his arm around Josiah and teleports them out leaving Atticus and Lola alone.

"We did it, Lola! We have Josiah. He is safe!" He throws his arms around her, pulling her body closer to his. He places his hands on her face and looks into her eyes. Atticus's eyes are filled with water, Lola has never seen him so happy. They hear the popping sound of Kevin's return, he releases Lola's face and pulls away. Just before Kevin teleports then from the field, Lola sees Atticus wipe one of his cheeks with his fingers.

*

Kevin teleports them into a bedroom, with walls that are covered in a floral-patterned wallpaper.

"We are at my house. My wife has gone to visit her parents." *'His wife, my great-great-grandmother.'*

"Athena thought it would be more accommodating for Josiah whilst he heals." they look at Josiah who is resting on a double bed covered in a plain, lace frilled duvet. Atticus seats himself down onto the bed next to his brother, he looks up at Kevin.

"I need to stay with him. Lola too."

Kevin looks between them all.

"Well, there is plenty of room. I will see what Athena says." And with a pop, Kevin teleports out of the bedroom.

*

"They want to stay," Kevin says immediately to Athena after landing in Atticus old room at the public house. Athena carries on folding some clothes and packing them into a suitcase, which looks new.

"I thought they might want to. It could be a good idea. In your house they would be safe, they could train, and Lola would be able to help ease Josiah's pain when it is needed." Athena turns to face Kevin, *he is just as handsome now, as he was when they were together; '1939, we would have been separated for almost five years now.'*

"Have you told Katherine yet? About what you are?" The last time Athena had seen Kevin was when he had told her about his engagement to Katherine; he had not told her then what he was, a Nephilim. His silence answers her question, she turns to continue to pack the clothes she had purchased to replace the ones that had been taken from Josiah by the Nazis. "What if she returns home earlier than expected and finds them mid-training? It could blow their cover, put them in harm's way."

"She won't. She will not leave, not until her mother has passed and the funeral has taken place," he replies.

"Okay. Yes, they can stay if you have room?"

"I have plenty of room," he reassures her. Athena closes the case and hands it to Kevin, along with Atticus's suitcase.

"Atticus and Josiah will be needing these. I will bring

171

Lola's when I check in on Josiah later." Athena informs him. Kevin nods and teleports out.

Athena presses a button on her communicator, Apollo's face appears projecting in front of her.

"Was the mission successful?"

"Yes. Josiah is now safe and sound in Kevin's house."

"How is he?"

"I think it is going to take some time before we have the Josiah we know back. I am going to ask Lola to speak to him. Josiah trusts her, and cares about her. Whatever else he went through in there; if he's going to confide in anyone it will be her."

"Not Atticus?" Apollo responds.

"No. He and Atticus are not as close as they used to be," she says with a tone of sadness lining her voice.

"Josiah is not the only reason why I am contacting you. I was hoping you could advise me on a situation that has developed, with Lola."

"What situation is that?" he asks her, urging her to continue.

"Lola and Atticus's bond with each other has developed to a level beyond what we thought possible."

"What do you mean?"

"'Child Atticus' it appears, reached out to her from the past."

"I don't understand?"

"Lola somehow manipulated her frequency whilst she was asleep. Her conscious travelled and took over her body in her life as Eurydice. It appears Atticus may have done the same when he was a child, but instead of travelling back in time, he travelled forward, witnessing a possible future timeline with

Lola. He then somehow placed himself into one of Lola's dreams when he was a child, informing her of that future timeline, the future he saw of them together." She waits as Apollo processes the information.

"Hmm. Have you spoken to father about this?"

"No. I thought I would speak to you first, see if you knew anything about this ability," she replies.

"I mean Cronus possessed the ability to travel through time, to the past and the future without using dolmens, so there is an ability where that is possible. And Morpheus had the ability to hijack dreams, so again there is an ability to do that. Since we are all connected, the chances are that these abilities could have been passed down to Atticus and Lola. Maybe because of their past connection, the way their relationship ended in that lifetime, with the two abilities combined, it is logical that their subconscious would try and find a way to re-connect with each other. During dream state our subconscious takes control, and whilst we dream, as you know; all conscious momentum, all resistance stops, therefore making it easier for our subconscious to travel," Apollo explains.

"Should we be worried?"

"I don't think so, not right now anyway. What about Atticus? Has he mentioned anything about taking over a 'past him' consciousness? Or a child him visiting Lola?" Athena shakes her head.

"No. Just Lola, and just the times I have shared with you," she tells him reassuringly.

"Then no, I do not think it is anything we need to be concerned about for now. Was there anything else?" Apollo asks her. Athena shakes her head.

"Okay, keep me posted on Josiah's health and send

Atticus, Lola, and Kevin my love," Apollo tells her before ending their call.

*

Kevin teleports back into the bedroom where he left Josiah, Lola, and Atticus. Atticus takes the two suitcases from him.

"Athena said you could both stay. Josiah, Athena has brought you some new clothes since..." Josiah finishes Kevin's sentence.

"The Nazis took mine."

"Yes."

"Where is mine?" Lola asks.

"Athena said she will bring yours later with her when she checks in on Josiah." Kevin smiles at Josiah.

"You're already looking much better Josiah. I am sure it won't be long before you are fully back to your usual self," he says positively.

"I will give you three some alone time. I am sure you have lots to talk about. I have some stew left over in the monitor-top. I will heat some up for you, I'm sure you are all completely famished." Lola looks between Atticus and Josiah: '*I should give them some time together.*'

"I will help you." Lola stands and follows Kevin out of the bedroom.

Atticus remains seated on the bed next to his brother; they sit in silence for a few moments.

"You must be tired. Would you like me to leave you alone?" Atticus says.

"No!" Josiah shouts, grabbing his brother's hand.

"Don't leave me," he says in panic. Atticus takes his

brother's hands in his.

"Okay. I promise I won't leave you. Not until you can't stand seeing the sight of me." Atticus says light-heartedly. Atticus stands, walks around the bed and stretches out on the bed next to Josiah.

"Do you want to talk about it?"

They sit next to each other in silence until Josiah speaks.

"The walls reminded me of the passage we escaped through, you know... when the King's men came for ma. It made me think about her, about aunt Anne." Josiah looks at his brother.

"Do you ever think about what would have happened if father hadn't died when we were children? Not until we were old enough to take care of ourselves. What our lives would have been like? Being raised by mother and father, instead of Athena? What we would have become? What do you think it would have been like?"

Atticus considers his brother's words, imagining what it would have been like, *No Lola, a world without Lola.* The thought ties knots in his stomach. Lola, who makes him want to be a better person, a better man. He thinks about their father, their mother and what their life was like when he and his brothers, and Henri, and their aunt Anne all lived under one roof. Well, for the majority of the time. He thinks about their father, how challenging it was for him, living two lives. He thinks about their mother, how gentle, strong, and loving she was. He thinks about what it was like being raised by Athena; she loved them and cared for them as much as she could have, but he always felt like something was missing. Until Lola entered their lives, he had always felt like something was missing.

"I used to think about all of that, and frequently. But then as I grew older, the more I travelled around the world, the more people I met, people I never would have met if we had stayed. I realised why things happened the way that they did. Looking back now I understand. I still think about ma and pa. They will always be our mother and father, I will always love them, and I will always be grateful for how much they loved and cared for us. But if we had stayed there, grown up there, then we would never have met the people that are in our lives now, the people we have met now. The people in our lives, that have come to be precious to us. I cannot imagine a life without them in it." Josiah looks at Atticus with affection.

"You're talking about Lola?"

Lola enters the room carrying a tray with three bowls of heated stew and some crusty bread rolls and butter. She looks between Atticus and Josiah; she knows she has interrupted them during a private moment.

"Sorry. I can leave these and come back later if you would like?" she says awkwardly.

"Not at all. I am famished, and what else could possibly make me feel better than eating some delicious food with the company of a beautiful woman?"

*

Kevin is finishing up on the dishwashing when he hears the knock on the front door. When he answers it, Athena, Lachesis, and Atropos are standing on his front porch. He steps aside, inviting them in.

"Lachesis and Atropos have located Clotho."

"Should I get the others?" he replies.

"Not yet," Athena says as she walks past Kevin.

Lachesis, Atropos, and Kevin follow Athena into the front lounge, they seat themselves on the matching olive-green sofa and armchair set.

"She is staying in an inn on the outskirts of Warsaw," Lachesis says.

"So, what's our next step?" Kevin asks.

"Lachesis and Atropos are going to travel to Warsaw ahead of us. Josiah cannot be moved until his feet have healed."

"But that could take weeks," Kevin comments.

"Atticus is a spellcaster, and Lola has access to healing abilities. Hopefully with their help, it will speed up the healing process."

"How has he been?" Athena asks him.

"Atticus has not left his side. I tried to suggest that he takes a few minutes for himself, but he's determined to not leave Josiah's side."

"Let me speak to him," Athena suggests.

*

Josiah, Atticus, and Lola look towards the bedroom door. Athena enters.

"Athena!" Josiah says with a tone of joy and hopefulness in his voice.

"Thank you for the clothes."

"You are very welcome," Athena says with a smile.

"How are you feeling?" she asks him with concern.

"Atticus and Lola have been making me laugh with all their stories."

"Sounds like you're doing much better. But I must steal

177

Atticus away from you for a few minutes. You don't mind, do you?" Athena asks Josiah. Josiah looks between Atticus and Athena with uncertainty.

"I'm here," Lola says cheerfully to Josiah, taking his hands in hers.

"Okay."

"I won't be long. I promise," Atticus reassures Josiah. Athena nods at Lola with a smile; *'she wants me to change into Panacea and heal Josiah some more.'* Atticus follows Athena out of the bedroom.

"Atticus doesn't know about my special ability," Lola informs Josiah.

"Athena wants me to change into Panacea and heal you some more. Atticus cannot know."

"Why doesn't she want Atticus to know?"

"It's best that as few people know about my shapeshifting ability as possible. Athena says, the more people that find out about my ability, the more danger it puts me and those I care about in." she says with the utmost seriousness.

"But she felt it was okay for me to know?" "Josiah, I had to provide you with some emergency healing, or we wouldn't have been able to rescue you from that hell," she says stubbornly.

"Kevin knows, Lachesis knows, Atropos knows. Everybody working this mission knows, except for Atticus. Keeping him in the dark is unfair!" he says protectively.

"Lachesis, and Atropos do not know, only you, Kevin, and Athena know. We had to tell Kevin as he was the one placed in charge with bringing me my clothes, so I could change out of the uniform. I have to do what Athena says, and right now she doesn't want me to tell Atticus."

"Lola it's your life, your ability. It's not Athena's choice who to tell and who not to tell, it is yours, and yours alone," he argues.

"You are right. It is my choice, but my choice right now is to trust that Athena knows what she is doing."

"I thought you cared about Atticus?" he says to her challenging her decision not to tell him.

"I do. Which is why I don't want him to know. If I could have avoided telling you I would have. From what I have been told so far; by having the shapeshifting ability, it not only puts myself in danger, but also everyone who I care about. I would rather keep you and Atticus safe than put your lives in danger."

"Lola. Atticus and I are skilled Nephilim, we can take care of ourselves, we both want to protect you. How can we protect you if we don't know what danger could occur?"

"Well like you said, it's my choice who to tell and who not to tell."

Josiah cares about Lola profoundly, but sometimes her stubbornness drove him crazy. He watches her as she walks to the foot of the bed and sits herself down next to his feet. Lola closes her eyes and pictures herself changing into Panacea. She feels the familiar warmth spread through her, the tugging and pulling of her insides as her outer appearance transforms into the appearance of Panacea. She opens her eyes and looks at Josiah, his jaw slightly lowered in awe again of watching her change in front of him.

"I don't think I will ever get used to that," Lola holds out her hands, palms facing the soles of Josiah's feet. She takes a deep breath in and then exhales, feeling the warmth of Panacea's healing energy flooding through her, passing from her and into Josiah's bandaged feet.

179

Chapter Twelve

Lola focuses on the healing energy continuously flowing through her, and then out through her hands. She had discovered that she likes the feeling of healing energy flowing through her, she found it therapeutic.

"What was is like growing up outside of the Nephilim world?" he asks her curiously.

"What do you mean?"

"What kind of things did you do?"

Lola thinks back to her childhood, it was nothing out of the ordinary. There was nothing that made it any different from most childhoods.

"I don't know. My parents were like everyone else's. Except I remember thinking once how my parents were more open minded than most parents. They thought out of the box."

"In what way were they more open minded?" she thinks back to one of her favourite games that she used to play whenever it rained, how differently they reacted to her playing in the rain, than other parents.

"You know the reflections you see in puddles?" she asks him.

"Yes."

"When I was around five or six years old, I used to pretend they were glimpses into other worlds, other dimensions. When I jumped into them, I pretended they were portals into those other worlds. When I jumped out on the other side, I pretended that I suddenly possessed superpowers and I would go exploring. My parents always played along, they would introduce challenges like meeting a nemesis, and we would imagine fighting them with our superpowers. Other parents would try to convince them that encouraging that kind of imagination in me was not good for me mentally. They used to tell them it would lead me to becoming a dreamer and dreamers never end up doing well in life. They always end up living a penniless life of unemployment. All that did was make them encourage it more. I remember looking at the other kids' parents in the playground, they would always be on their phones, or gossiping. My parents were the opposite; they were always coming up with games for us to play, or they would read to me a lot. When I started to have my dreams, other parents would have sent their child to see a child psychologist . My parents sat me down and tried to help me understand them." she looks up at Josiah and smiles.

"What was it is like being raised in the Nephilim world?"

"There was a lot of secrecy. We were only allowed to make friends; to be ourselves around other Nephilim families that lived in our community. We weren't allowed to go and play with other children. Because of that, we were often called names by the other children we had classes with. Our Father and Mother started teaching us how to fight as soon as were able to walk. The number of times I wanted to use our fighting skills when a child started on us, knowing it was forbidden frustrated me. I was a nightmare child, I was always the fighter, Atticus was always the lover."

"Sounds lonely."

A knock at the door breaks the silence. Lola had just about

finished the change back into herself when Atticus and Athena re-enter the room.

*

Atticus walks over and seats himself back down next to Josiah.

"See. I told you I wouldn't be long," he tells him.

"Athena thinks it's a good idea to practice my spellcasting ability on you by casting a healing spell. What do you think?"

"I think that is a splendid idea!" Josiah responds enthusiastically.

"Lola. You look like you could do with a nap. Why don't you go and take one?" Athena suggests to her. Lola smiles and exits the room.

"How do we start?" Atticus asks Athena.

"Go and sit at the bottom of his feet; hold your hands out in front of you, palms facing towards the soles of his feet." Atticus does as Athena instructed. Athena seats herself down onto the bed near Josiah's ankles.

"Do I need to take off the bandages?"

"No. The spell should work through them," She reassures him.

"Now what?" Atticus says asking for his next instruction.

"I want you to close your eyes. Start taking some deep breaths in and out," she instructs him. Atticus closes his eyes and takes a deep breath in and then exhales, repeating the process along with continuing to listen to Athena's voice.

"Feel your breath turn into a bright gold colour, feel it fill every nook and cranny within you. Then as you exhale, I want you to imagine you are breathing that bright gold out, allowing it to flow around you. Feel your whole body release any

182

tension and relax. When you feel like you and your body have connected to that bright gold energy, repeat these words. 'Sana manus mea tecum'. 'Sana manus mea tecum'. 'Sana manus mea tecum'."

Atticus joins Athena in chanting the spell after the fourth time.

"Open your eyes." she instructs him. Atticus slowly opens his eyes; he is in awe of the sight of a golden ray of light beaming from his hands into Josiah's feet. He looks up at his brother and smiles.

"How does it feel?" Atticus asks him.

"It feels like when the sun is warm, and you can feel the warmth of the sun beaming onto your skin."

*

It isn't until almost one o'clock that Josiah finally wakes up after sleeping twelve hours straight. He hears a knock on the door. and Athena enters.

"Oh, good, you are awake. How did you sleep?" He looks at the clock on his bedside table.

"I can't remember the last time I slept twelve hours straight," he answers.

"I can." Athena says seating herself down next to him.

"It was when you were thirteen and caught a severe case of the chicken pox." She reminds him.

"Ah yes! That was when I decided I would never look at oats the same way again." Athena laughs.

"So, porridge is off the cards for lunch then? What would you like? Kevin went and bought some eggs, beans, and bacon. What about a good old-fashioned fry up?" she suggests.

"Yes please," he says with more excitement than she had ever seen someone have over a fry up.

Half an hour later, Athena arrives back in the room carrying his fry up on a tray, a glass of orange juice and Lola and Atticus in tow.

"Are we having a party?" Athena places the tray of food onto Josiah's lap.

"I just thought this would be a good time to update you with what is happening with Clotho." Atticus and Lola take a seat on the bed.

"Lachesis and Atropos have located her, she's staying at an inn on the outskirts of Warsaw. We: Lachesis, Atropos, Kevin, and I have decided the best thing for us to do now is to allow Lachesis and Atropos to travel to Warsaw ahead of us; to do some digging into what Clotho's plans might be, and to arrange our accommodation, so that when we arrive everything would have already been prepared for our arrival."

"It sounds like a good plan," Josiah says whilst munching on some bacon.

"It will give me a chance to train a bit before we leave," Josiah says to them.

"With the help of Atticus, and his healing spellcasting ability, I am healing much faster Josiah smiles at his brother in gratitude.

"Okay, well if there is anything you need just shout," Athena says to Josiah. Atticus lets out a yawn.

"I think I need a nap. You don't mind do you Josiah, if I leave you in the capable hands of Lola here, whilst I take a nap?"

"The bags under your eyes have turned into sacks." Josiah says teasing him. Athena and Atticus leave the room leaving Josiah and Lola alone: *'Excellent, I can give Josiah another session.'*

184

*

Atticus finds himself standing in a grand hall. Six tall, white marble pillars line the sides of the room. He looks down at the floor which is tiled with large gold panels. A man with a long, flowing white beard and white hair down to his shoulders enters. Atticus recognises the man immediately, the man is Zeus, he must be in Olympus. A much younger Apollo and Athena follow Zeus into the room. In one hand Apollo is carrying a lyre. Clutching Apollo's other hand is a young boy around the age of twelve. The boy's appearance resembles Apollo; his hair is dark, his skin olive. A moment of de'ja'vu sweeps of Atticus '*The boy is me. I know it, I feel it.*' Athena looks how she always looks during his past-life regression sessions in learning how to control his emotions when dreaming of this life. Zeus waves his hands around and mumbles something, but Atticus doesn't hear what Zeus had said. A throne and three smaller chairs appear in the room. The chairs, although smaller than the throne, match the throne's décor. All of them have red velvet cushioning, surrounded by a gold frame.

"My dear son, happy twelfth birthday. Do you like your present?" Apollo asks the boy (past-life Atticus as a child)

"Yes father. Thank you," the boy replies. Apollo holds out his arms offering a fatherly hug. Apollo brings one of the smaller chairs closer to him and instructs the boy to sit down.

"Would you like me to teach you how to play it?" Apollo asks the boy as he passes him the lyre, he nods. Apollo stands from his chair and walks to behind the boys chair. The new information starts to sink in and hits Atticus like a ton of bricks; '*I was Apollo's son. Apollo was once my father. Why didn't he tell me?'* Atticus continues to watch Apollo with past life him. Atticus had never seen Apollo look at someone with as much love, appreciation, and adoration before. He watches himself in this life start to play the strikingly beautiful instrument. It's music like Atticus has never heard before; *'It's beautiful'.*

"Atticus, Atticus," he hears his name being called to him. He feels the familiar pull of being pulled to wake. He opens his eyes to find Athena standing over him. He pulls up the cover towards his chin to cover his bare torso.

"Meeting. Downstairs," she simply says before turning on her heels and exiting the room.

*

Kevin—*'my great-great-grandfather'.* Lola still found it surreal that she was having the chance to meet him, get to know him; is sitting alone in the armchair in the lounge. Lola sinks herself into the sofa.

"Where is everyone else?" she looks at the television, an old black and white movie is being shown on it.

"Lachesis, Athena, and Atropos are having a meeting in the kitchen. I'm guessing Atticus is still napping?" he answers. Lola notices a black and white photograph of him and Katherine; *'my great great grandmother',* on their wedding day, on the mantelpiece.

"What is she like?" she asks him, looking at the photograph.

"Katherine? She is stubborn like you, but I think you take more after my mother. She was very much a warrior, just like you are. I'm not sure if Athena has told you this but Katherine, your

186

great, great grandmother is not one of us. I haven't told her yet what I am."

"Doesn't that make things difficult? Your wife not knowing what you are?"

"Lola, living a life of a Nephilim is wonderful in many ways. But it also has its downfalls; it is dangerous, and most Nephilim do not have the luxury of living a long life, like most non-Nephilim. I wanted children, and I wanted to be able to give my children a chance to live a long, safe life. So, I made the choice that the best way to do that was to marry a non-Nephilim woman and leave this world behind."

"But you do *love* her, don't you?"

"I do." Lola feels hesitation coming from him, he wants to tell her something else but doesn't know how to.

"But…" she says, edging him on to continue.

Atticus enters the room.

"You're awake. How was your nap?" Kevin asks him. '*He was about to tell me something important,* 'enters Lola's mind.

"Where's Athena? She wanted me to meet her down here for a meeting"

"She's in the kitchen. Are you okay?"

"Everything is fine," Atticus says before exiting the room.

*

Athena, Lachesis, and Atropos are all sitting around the breakfast table when Atticus enters the kitchen.

"Atticus. Finally!" Athena says, acknowledging Atticus's entrance.

"Athena, I need to speak you about something, something important."

187

"Atticus, we're in the middle of the meeting. Can't it wait?"

"No. Not really," he says. Athena dismisses Lachesis, and Atropos from the meeting.

Atticus seats himself on the bench opposite her.

"I had another dream. Athena why didn't you, or Apollo tell me that I used to be his son?" They sit in silence for a few moments before Athena answers his question.

"Atticus this is something you should really discuss with Apollo, not me."

"Apollo isn't here. I don't need the full story right now, just the reason. You can tell me that." Athena takes a moment to think before she speaks.

"So, he wouldn't run the risk of changing anything," Athena replies.

"What do you mean?"

"Any knowledge you gain from knowing what happened in a past life, can affect any decisions we make in a current one. And that is not a good thing, because there is a reason why every life needs to be different. Look Atticus, this really is something you should be discussing with Apollo. Just trust in that he never mentioned it to you before for good reason. However, I am sure if you wish to speak to him about it now, he would be more than happy to do so. Now that you are getting better at separating lives, and understanding that you cannot allow what you experienced, what you felt in a previous life, influence your experience, what you feel in this one." Atticus considers Athena's words.

"Okay. I will talk to Apollo about it when we return to our time."

"Am I essential to this meeting? I need to go and check on

Josiah, I need to check his wounds. You said we should be able to see if the healing spell has worked by now."

"No, you are not essential to this meeting. I can catch you up later. Go and check on your brother"

*

When Atticus enters Josiah's room, Lola is still in there with him, stretched out beside him.

"I've come to see if any of the healing sessions have worked."

"Be my guest!" Josiah replies.

Atticus walks over to the foot of the bed, seating himself at the bottom of Josiah's feet and unravels the bandages that are protecting his feet. Atticus looks between Josiah and Lola and smiles. Lola joins him in checking Josiah's feet; when she too, sees his feet, she smiles. Atticus chuckles and looks at his brother again.

"The slashes have completely scabbed over and are almost completely healed," he says. Josiah pulls up his feet to have a look at them, a big grin appears across his face. He stands up and starts to walk around the room.

"I can walk! I feel no pain!" He does a little jump.

"We should tell the others. With Josiah now healed, and able to walk, we should be able to head to Warsaw soon."

"Lola. Josiah can only just walk. Don't you think we should wait until the scabs have fallen off and the wounds have completely healed?"

"Lola is right," Josiah says to Atticus.

"A couple more healing sessions should leave me completely healed enabling us all to travel to Warsaw and

189

complete the mission we were all originally sent here to complete."

"Are you sure?" Atticus asks his brother.

"Positive. The completion of our mission has been hindered for far too long already. We shall tell the others that I will be ready to travel to Warsaw tomorrow.

"Atticus let's begin another healing session, shall we?"

"Lola, go and inform the others with the good news" Lola leaves the brothers alone to go and inform the others as Atticus instructed. As Atticus prepares to do another healing session on Josiah, Josiah can tell something is weighing heavily on Atticus's mind.

"Do you honestly feel you're ready to carry on with the mission?" Atticus asks breaking the silence.

"Is that what you're worried about? Or is there something else weighing heavily on that mind of yours?" An awkward silence occurs as Atticus thinks about how to bring up his thoughts about what he has been sensing between his brother and Lola.

"I've been thinking about you and Lola," Atticus finally says biting the bullet

"Myself and Lola?"

Atticus continues to heal Josiah's feet in between talking. "Yes, since we rescued you from the Nazi's, it's obvious that something has happened between you both. I see the way you look at her, the way she sometimes is around you" Josiah lets out a sigh of grief.

"I kissed her," he simply states.

"When we were in the underground tunnel, I kissed her. It was nothing, a moment led from the joy of being rescued"

"Are you sure?" Atticus asks.

"Yes. Even if you don't admit it, I know you have feelings for her. I just wonder why you're not admitting it, because I know you know she feels the same way about you. Personally, I think you're mad. If you weren't my brother…" Josiah stops before he can continue as Lola re-enters the room.

"Sorry to interrupt, Kevin is waiting for us in the garden" Lola informs Atticus.

Chapter Thirteen

The train from Kielce to Warsaw was busier than they had anticipated. Luckily, they were all able to get their seats together. By the time they reached Warsaw, the sun had already started to set. Lachesis, and Atropos are waiting at the station ready to collect them.

"Josiah, you are looking well," Lachesis says to him, as they step down off the train.

"I feel much better, thanks to the healing treatments," Josiah says smiling gleefully.

As Lola looks around Warsaw; making their way to the inn they had made their reservations with, it feels much bigger than Kielce, the streets are wider, the buildings further apart, not cramped together like they were in Kielce.

Beep… Beep… Beep, they all turn around to see who was bibbing. A Nazi truck is driving towards them. They hear a sudden scream and spin around to see Josiah on the floor screaming 'No' and crying. Atticus and Lola are immediately on their knees next to him.

"Josiah! Josiah!" Atticus and Lola shout at him, attempting to bring him back from wherever he has gone, he's clearly having a flashback.

*

As Josiah lays on his side facing the cold, wet stones of his cell, he hears the familiar sound of heavy footsteps of boots approaching him, stopping outside his cell. Josiah hears the Nazi exhale and bend down to pick up the food tray that was left for him outside of his cell, the food untouched. the footsteps leave, only to return moments later accompanied by a second pair of heavy booted footsteps Josiah turns as he hears the cell door open.

"It is disrespectful to us to not eat the food we give to you." They drag him into one of the empty rooms.

"No. No you cannot do this to me again!" Josiah screams at them. It is the torture room.

"We warned you that if you do not play nice, you will be punished. You disrespect and reject our kindness in feeding you, so now you pay. Strap him down!" Two Nazi soldiers do as he requests and pull Josiah from the taller soldier and the shorter Nazi soldier and force him to face down onto the blood-stained table. They strap his wrists and ankles down, so the soles of his feet are facing upwards towards the ceiling. Josiah watches from the corner of his eye as the shorter of the two soldiers that had dragged him into the room hands the taller one a bullwhip. He continues to watch as the taller one walks to the foot end of the table. As he feels him trace the soles of his feet with the bullwhip, his body tenses.

"Maybe this will teach you some manners," the soldier continues to trace the whip over Josiah's soles back and forth in circular motions. He flinches, when the soldiers stops, he squeezes his eyes tight in preparation when he hears the whooshing sound of the whip making its way through the air; crack... crack. He can almost hear the sound of Lola's voice calling his name. Josiah opens his eyes, disorientated. Lola and

Atticus are kneeling down beside him.

*

"Help! Help!" the sound of a woman shouting for help in the distance distracts the Nazis, they do a three-point turn and head towards the screams of help.

"Josiah, Josiah." Lola and Atticus continue to say. He looks between them, they sigh with relief.

"What happened?" Josiah asks them dazed.

"You blacked out," Atticus informs him. They help him up.

"Are you okay?" Lola asks him. He looks around the group and nods.

"I'm fine. Just embarrassed."

"Are we far from the inn?" Athena asks Lachesis and Atropos.

"Just over a mile away," Atropos replies.

"Do you think you'll be okay to walk the rest of the way? Or would you prefer Kevin to teleport you there?" Athena asks Josiah.

"No. I'm fine. I don't know what happened, but I feel fine," Josiah replies wiping his wet cheeks with his fingers. Athena nods in understanding.

*

The inn is empty of guests when they arrive.

"I thought it would be busier?" Lola comments airing her thoughts.

"It's a Nephilim safe house. The only guests are Nephilim

who are under protection or passing through on missions." Lachesis informs her.

"Madame Sinclair!" Lola says in joy at the sight of Madame Sinclair behind the reception desk.

"I'm sorry have we met?" she asks Lola baffled by her sudden outburst.

"Lola," Athena pulls Lola over to one side and says softly, "That is Madame Sinclair from this time. She has not met you yet." Athena smiles at her. Lola turns to face Madame Sinclair.

"I'm sorry. You're right, we have not met. I'm a big fan of yours from hearing so many good things about you, and your styling skills." Lola smiles at her reassuringly, she looks her up and down.

"Well, if at any time you would like to go shopping, or in need of some assistance, I would be more than happy to assist you. Always up for helping out a fan," she says to Lola winking .

"That would be lovely!"

Madame Sinclair pulls out a drawer and pulls out various sets of keys.

"One twin room. I am guessing that is for these two handsome gentlemen," she says handing Atticus and Josiah the key to their room,

"And three more doubles," she says handing the remaining keys to Athena, Kevin, and Lola.

"I am afraid we are currently a bit short staffed, so I hope you do not mind if Lachesis, and Atropos show you to your rooms?"

"No need for that," Athena says to her. "I am sure we are all perfectly capable of finding our own rooms." They all nod in agreement and thank Madame Sinclair in turn, for her hospitality.

*

"I have been looking for you," Lola tells Josiah. He is sitting on a bench out in the garden. The garden is large, it consists of various types of flowers, in the centre of the garden stands a large marble statue of the sign that stands for Olympus. The sign for Olympus reminds Lola of the modern sign for the astrological sign of Libra, but without the line that runs across the bottom.

"What really happened earlier?" Lola asks him softly. "What did you see?"

"I didn't see anything," he replies.

"You know when you lie, your voice goes up a pitch."

"What did you see?" she asks him again.

"I care about you Josiah. I want to be there for you. But I cannot be there for you if you don't let me in." they sit in silence for a few moments as Lola waits patiently for his response.

"I had a flashback," is the first thing he says.

"I had a flashback to one of the times they came to my cell and dragged me to one of the torture rooms and lashed me," Lola goes to place her hand on the hand that was resting on his lap; but before she does, he pulls it away from her. He turns to face her.

"I don't want you to pity me," he says anxiously.

"I could never pity you."

"You two look cosy!" they turn to see Atticus approaching them. Josiah stands up to leave. "Everything okay?" Atticus

196

asks them.

"Everything is fine," Josiah replies.

"I'll see you tomorrow, Lola."

"Night Josiah, see you tomorrow." she smiles at him reassuringly.

"You don't have to leave on my account," Atticus informs him.

"I'm not. I'm just tired." Josiah replies before nodding and leaving Atticus and Lola alone in the garden.

"Is he okay?" Atticus asks her as he takes Josiah's place next to her on the bench.

"He went through a lot in there."

"I wish he would talk to me about it. Whenever I try to get him to open himself up to me about what happened in there, he changes the subject. We used to be so close, and now it feels like we're growing apart. It feels like I am losing him and everything I try, to regain that closeness, feels like I am pushing us apart even more. I miss him, Lola."

Lola reflects on the words that have just escaped Atticus's mouth. She thinks about how close they were when she had first met them, although complete opposites, they were inseparable. It is true what he has just said; they had grown apart.

"I think at some point, all siblings go through a time when they drift apart. I think that needs to happen in order to grow as individuals, especially with twins. But then when they reconnect; the bond is stronger than before. Atticus, you and your brothers, and Henri have already been through so much together. And during this mission, with Josiah being taken by the Nazis and tortured; I think he just needs some time. Even though it may feel like you have grown apart, you are still part of each other, and I think he misses you too. But right now, after what happened, I think he just needs some time. I am positive that he will come back to you, and he will open himself up to you again."

"I am sure you are right. I am sure after some time he will start to confide in me again. He will come back to me. Lola, whilst we were in Kielce, I had another dream. I was dreaming of memories again. I was a child. It was my birthday and Apollo was my father. I haven't told him yet that I know. I tried talking to Athena about it, but she said I should talk to him, but I'm not sure how to approach him."

"What would you like say to him?"

"I don't know. I mean I don't think him being my father in a past life has anything to do with this life. I'm just wondering why he never told me."

"Maybe like you, he thought there was no point mentioning it, if it has nothing to do with now." They sit in silence for a moment just looking at each other.

"Lola." They look up to see Athena walking towards them.

"Sorry. Am I interrupting something?" She asks as she notices their flushed faces.

"Actually yes, you are," Atticus replies. He turns his attention back to Lola, leans into her and says softly into her ear

"Why do we always seem to get interrupted at the most interesting moments?" He turns to look at Athena and sighs, then leans in and kisses Lola on the cheek, almost grazing his lips against hers. Lola always thought that when authors wrote in books, or a character in a film mentions time standing still in moments such as this, that it was fantasy. As Atticus's lips almost touched hers, it had felt like time had slowed right down to an almost a stop. She finds herself watching him as he walks back into the inn.

"Lola," Athena says bringing her out of the moment.

"Lola, I saw you talking to Josiah out here. Did he confide in you about what he experienced earlier?" She was more serious than Lola has ever seen her. *'She really does love and care about the Hardy boys.'*

"He did."

"What happened?"

"I'm sorry Athena, but only Josiah can tell you, when he feels he is ready," Lola replies loyally.

"You are a good friend to Josiah, and a loyal Nephilim. I understand and respect your loyalty to those you care about. But you would tell me, wouldn't you? If he were in any danger?" she asks Lola anxiously.

"Of course. I just feel as Josiah's friend, that I should respect his trust in me. But I promise you, if Josiah were to ever confide in me, anything which I felt could mean he were in any danger, mentally, physically, or otherwise, I will tell you."

"Okay," Athena simply replies.

*

When Atticus enters his and Josiah's room at the inn, Josiah is already changed and lying in bed, curled up facing the window. When they were given their room, Josiah was the first to claim the bed that was nearest to the window.

"Are you still awake?" Atticus asks him as he enters the room closing the door behind him, Even though Atticus knew he was, Josiah doesn't reply. Atticus exhales, changes into his pyjamas and brushes his teeth before climbing into his own bed.

"Night, Josiah!" Atticus shouts over to him. Still no reply. Atticus exhales and switches off his bedside lamp.

The sound of crying wakes Atticus up from his slumber.

"Josiah. Josiah," Atticus says as he scoops his brother into his arms.

"Shh. It's okay, it's okay," Atticus softly says to his brother, attempting to soothe him.

"I keep being back there. Keep feeling the pain as they continue to lash me. I keep hearing the other prisoners screams as I did when I heard them echo through the cell walls." Atticus pulls his brother closer to him and kisses the top of his head, consoling him.

*

Kevin, Lachesis, Atropos, Athena and Lola are already halfway through their breakfast plates that are piled with eggs, bacon, sausages, beans, and slices of toast, when Atticus and Josiah enter the breakfast room.

"Ah, Atticus, Josiah. I was just saying to Lola that it might be good for you three to go out tonight, let your hair down." Athena says updating Atticus and Josiah of the conversation.

"I thought we were not allowed to do such a thing; in case it has an impact on the timeline?" Atticus replies whilst spreading some marmalade onto his buttered toast.

"I thought about that. I figured as long as you do not interact with anyone else and only interact amongst yourselves, there is no reason why the timeline should be affected. There is a flyer on the noticeboard that the Polish pianist Józef Koffler will be playing in a bar tonight in the city. I think you three should go. I think a night of getting dressed up is just what you need before our mission tomorrow, and our journey back to Pentre Ifan. What do you think?" Athena asks them.

"If you think it will not impact the timeline, then I think you are right, a night out on the town could be just what we need!" Josiah replies.

"But we don't have anything to wear." Lola pitches in. Athena smiles.

"That can easily be sorted. I am sure Madame Sinclair would be more than happy to carry out her offer of taking you shopping. Kevin could take Josiah, and Atticus. What do you think Kevin?" Athena asks Kevin.

"I think I know a place," Kevin comments.

"Good. I shall speak to Madame Sinclair, and then after your training session this morning…"

"Training session?" Josiah says, interrupting Athena.

"Yes. I think it would be wise if you, Atticus, and Lola trained this morning. Kevin has offered to assist again." Athena says to them, smiling.

"It's been a while since you have all had the chance to practice your self-defence techniques and your abilities together. Tomorrow night we are executing our plan to capture Clotho. I thought it would be wise to have one last training session before we do so. Do you not agree?" Athena asks them.

"I think that is a very good idea." Josiah answers. Atticus glances at Lola, who looks worryingly at Josiah. Athena notices Atticus and Lola's uncertainty.

*

When Atticus and Lola enter the inn's garden, wearing their training gear ready for the training session, they are the first ones there.

"Do you think this is a good idea?"

"You mean because of Josiah?" Atticus replies.

"Yes. I mean you and I both know that he is not mentally ready for this."

"I agree, but maybe it will help. Maybe it will distract him allow him to place his focus onto something else, away from the memories of his time with the Nazis." I consider his words; maybe Atticus is right.

"I hope you are right," Lola says to him just before Kevin and Josiah exit the inn and walk towards them.

"Okay. Let's do fifteen minutes of warm up and then start with the self-defence techniques," Kevin instructs.

*

Lola is still wrapped in her towel from taking a shower after the training session when Athena knocks.

"Just one moment," She shouts before quickly pulling on one of the tea dresses that Madame Sinclair had packed for her.

"Come in!" Athena enters her room.

"How was Josiah?" she asks Lola instantaneously closing the door behind herself.

"Surprisingly okay. I think the training session helped distract him from the thoughts of his experience with the Nazis. I think going out tonight will also help. When he's being kept pre-occupied, he doesn't seem to be thinking about what

202

happened. He's more like his old self."

"Thank you, Lola, for being my eyes and ears. Madame Sinclair has agreed to take you shopping. She will be waiting for you in the dining room at one thirty. That should give you more than enough time to find something suitable for tonight. Also, would you mind joining me for a moment?"

"Okay," she says and follows Athena to Josiah and Atticus's room.

*

Atticus and Josiah are exiting their room, on their way to meet Kevin when they bump into Athena and Lola.

"Can I have word with you both quickly? I know you're on your way out, it won't take long. There is something I need to discuss with you, something important. I should have told you before we started this mission, but there was never a suitable time. And now we have reached a point where it cannot be delayed any longer." Athena says to Atticus, and Josiah. She instructs the two brothers, to go back to their room, ushering them in, instructing them and Lola to sit.

Once Lola, Atticus and Josiah are seated, they watch on as Athena starts pacing back and forth in the room. All three of them continue to sit in silence whilst waiting for Athena to speak. She finally stops pacing and turns to look at them all.

"A long, long, long time ago Zeus foretold that there were going to be a group of scientists that would come together. He foretold that this group of scientists were going to lead the Nephilim into extinction. He then foretold that Nephilim twin brothers, and a Nephilim girl were going to be born, and it would be these three Nephilim warriors that would grow up to be the salvation of the Nephilim race.

"He foretold that these three Nephilim warriors were going to be born to a Nephilim father and a Nephilim mother making them few of the remaining full bloodied Nephilim. He also foretold that they would be incarnations of previous prophets. Atticus, Josiah have you ever wondered why it was necessary for you to survive the attack from the King's men? Why Apollo and I had to rescue you, your brother, and cousin? It was because when you were born Zeus knew you were the brothers from the prophecy. And you Lola, when you were born and started to have the dreams of your past life, Zeus knew that you were the female warrior from the same prophecy. It was because of this that you three were the chosen ones for this mission." They sit in silence processing the bomb of information Athena has just delivered onto them.

"So, let me get this straight. The group of scientists; Zeus thinks that this is the S.G.E.?" Atticus asks her.

"He doesn't think, he knows," Athena replies.

"And he thinks that Josiah, Lola, and I are the three Nephilim from the prophecy?" he continues to ask.

"Yes. Although again he doesn't think, he knows," Athena informs them.

"But how can he be sure that it is us?" Lola asks.

"Your past links with Atticus, and Josiah confirms it."

"My past link with Atticus, and Josiah?"

"Yes. The dreams that both you and Atticus have of your past lives. They are dreams of your past life together when you were lovers. We expect that soon enough, you will also start dreaming of your past life with Josiah, as will he." Athena looks between them. Josiah is next to speak.

"So, what you're saying is that both Atticus and I have

had past lives with Lola?" Atticus and Josiah both turn to look at Lola and at each other.

"Yes. And you and Atticus have also been brothers before too." *This cannot be happening;* Lola stands up.

"I have to go. I need to meet Madame Sinclair. Sorry." Lola rushes out of the room in haste leaving Athena, Josiah, and Atticus alone in the room. As she shuts the door behind herself and walks hastily towards the stairs, she has to stop. Lola's heart feels like it's about to burst.

*

Madame Sinclair is already waiting for Lola in the dining area.

"Ah there you are. I was starting to think you had changed your mind," she says in her heavy French accent; "Is everything okay? You seem flustered?" she asks Lola as she arrives.

"I'm fine. Looking forward to finding a dress for tonight." Lola says smiling Madame Sinclair reassuringly.

Madame Sinclair takes Lola to a small boutique located down a pebble stoned alleyway in the city. As Lola steps through the shop's surrounding area, a warmth, spreads over her. Madame Sinclair, as if reading Lola's mind informs her,

"It's the shield."

"The shield?" Lola asks her.

"Yes. The shield. Only Nephilim, or gods can enter this store." She continues to inform Lola.

"What happens if a non-Nephilim tries to enter?" Lola asks her curiously.

"That is not possible. The shop is surrounded by shields hiding it from them. However, and very rarely, when someone of non-Nephilim blood does see it, if they try to enter, they are jolted with electricity that causes them to bounce off and lose partial memory."

"Isn't that kind of dangerous?"

"Not really. It may cause some discomfort, that is all." Madame Sinclair walks over to the reception desk and rings the bell, moments later Aphrodite appears.

"Madame Sinclair!" Aphrodite says gleefully as she embraces Madame Sinclair and kisses her on both cheeks. Aphrodite turns to face Lola.

"And who is this?" she asks Madame Sinclair extending her hand out for Lola to shake; Lola could have sworn she also just sneakily winked at her.

"This is Marie Dudek, she is just passing through with Athena." introducing them. Lola shakes Aphrodite's hand.

"Marie needs an evening gown. She will be attending the Józef Koffler piano concert tonight."

"Well then, let's have a look at you! Hourglass. Hmm I think a V-neck neckline is definitely the right place to start, perhaps in silk, and colours in shades of dark blue, or green to compliment her beautiful auburn hair, and those stunning curves." Lola feels herself blush at Aphrodite's kind compliments.

"Okay. Marie, Madame Sinclair. Please take a seat on the chaise longue, I will pick out some dresses and be right back." Madame Sinclair, and Lola does as Aphrodite instructs, taking a seat on the red velvet chaise longue.

Five minutes later Aphrodite returns with a selection of long dresses in dark blue, different shades of green, along with a couple of silver and gold dresses.

"Please stand," Aphrodite instructs Lola. She does as she

is asked and stands. Aphrodite holds up each dress to Lola, one by one, occasionally handing one for Madame Sinclair to take. Once Aphrodite has finished holding the dresses up to Lola, she takes the chosen dresses from Madame Sinclair and hands them to her.

"Either one of these should work." Aphrodite walks over to one of the pale-pink painted wooden doors and opens it.

"This is the changing room. Please come out after each dress and show us." All the dresses are made of silk, are V-necks and have flowing mermaid silhouettes, flowing down to almost touching the floor. The first dress Lola chose to try on is the gold one; when she exits the changing room to show Aphrodite and Madame Sinclair, they both shake their heads in unison.

"No. Next," Aphrodite simply says. This continues until the fourth dress which consists of a low back also; it is emerald green in colour.

"Yes!" they both shout out in unison and jump up enthusiastically from sitting on the chaise longue.

"One moment!" Aphrodite says, appearing moments later with a pearl necklace, matching bracelet, and a pair of black t-strap high heels.

"You will also be needing these," she says handing Lola the items.

"The necklace, bracelet and shoes are my own so be careful with them. Madame Sinclair will bring them back to me once you have finished with them. You look beautiful Marie! Doesn't she look wonderful?" Aphrodite asks Madame Sinclair.

"She is very beautiful; the brothers will not be able to take their eyes off of you!"

"Brothers?" Aphrodite says teasingly.

"Marie has two admirers that are brothers," She informs Aphrodite.

"They are good friends, that is all," Lola says, correcting her. Aphrodite chuckles.

"Ah. Okay." Lola walks back into the changing room and changes back into the clothes she came in. When Lola exits, Madame Sinclair is already at the desk paying.

"Athena gave me the money, I hope you do not mind that I went ahead and paid for the dress?"

"I shall have to thank Athena when I see her."

*

Lola is just slipping on the dress when she hears a knock. She answers the door, standing in the corridor is Athena.

"Wow, Lola, you look beautiful. I thought you might need some help getting ready?"

"Actually yes, some help would be good. I'm having trouble with the zipper."

Athena closes the door behind her. Lola holds up her arm so Athena can reach the zipper.

"Thank you."

"I also thought I should check in to see how you are doing; after hearing about the prophecy," Athena asks Lola cautiously.

"I am not quite sure the information has sunken in yet."

"Well, when you are ready to talk more about it. I will be more than happy to discuss it further with you."

Lola smiles at her through the reflection in the mirror. She passes Athena the pearl necklace to do up for her.

"Lola, I cannot believe what a beautiful, brave young woman you have become since meeting you. Your mother would be so proud of you!" After the comment, Athena embraces Lola in a tight hug.

"Ready for your big night out?"

Atticus, and Josiah are already waiting for Lola in the reception area. They are wearing matching evening suits; except Atticus's jacket is white, and Josiah's is black. They are the most handsome, beautiful men Lola had ever seen. They took her breath away. As Lola approaches them, they each offer her an arm..

"You look beautiful" Josiah whispers into her ear.

Chapter Fourteen

Lola did not expect to feel the sadness she felt stepping into the piano bar. They look around at the men in their evening suits, the women in their elegant evening dresses; the thought of knowing what was about to happen to them, witnessing them all laughing, chatting amongst themselves, enjoying their evening as they listen to the pianist Koffler run his fingers over the white grand piano keys; not knowing about the disruption and tragedy that was about to happen to them, pulled the strings of Lola's heart.

"Are you okay, Lola?" Josiah softly asks her. She gives him her 'I'm fine' smile.

"Follow me, please," one of the waiters says to them, they follow him to one of the round tables that is covered in a white lace tablecloth. Atticus pulls out a chair for Lola to sit; after they take their seats, the waiter that showed them to their seats hands them the drinks menu. Another waiter offers Atticus and Josiah a cigar, from a silver tray of cigars that he was carrying, they politely decline his offer, the waiter makes his way over to the next table. When the first waiter returns, they order three gin and tonics.

"He's incredible, isn't he?" Josiah says breaking the silence between them all.

"He is," Lola replies . The waiter returns with their drinks, Lola takes a sip, and continues to glance around at the men and women that surround them.

"Lola, what's wrong? We are in a bar, listening to beautiful music, dressed up and I don't think I have ever seen you looking so miserable. Why are you so sad?" Lola places her drink onto the table.

"Everybody is happy, living their lives, enjoying themselves. It's, it's hard, knowing that in a few months, their lives are going to change in one of the most tragic of ways. They are all happy, living their lives blissfully. There is an abundance of joy, love, and appreciation in this room, and in a few months the Nazis will completely take over. Some of them will die, or their loved ones will be taken from them, their children, siblings, parents. Fear, and hate is about to take over, and there is nothing we can do to warn them, to help them. Athena said it herself; it is a risk to even be here, in this bar. If we say, or do anything, interact with anyone other than ourselves, we could run the risk of changing the timeline. I was so excited at the thought of travelling here, to experience life in another time, to see the architecture, the people. I never thought seeing them happy, knowing that was all about to change, and not being able to do anything about it would be so hard." Atticus places his hand over the hand that is resting on her leg.

"Me neither," he says softly. Josiah's eyes have glazed over, his mind has drifted, Lola places her spare hand onto his.

"I am sorry, Josiah. I didn't mean to remind you of your time spent with the Nazis."

He smiles and places his other hand on top of hers affectionately.

"It's okay, Lola. You are right, it is hard seeing these people happy, knowing what they are all about to go through.

Knowing there is nothing we can do, knowing that we are lucky that we get to leave here before it happens." Josiah picks up his gin and tonic.

"I think we should toast to them, their bravery. To bravery." They toast, clinking their glasses.

"Now, I think we should embrace the rest of the evening, it is not very often one gets to be in the presence, and witness one the most famous Polish composers," Josiah says, standing offering Lola his hand, inviting her to dance.

"Shall we?"

*

The evening flies by fast. Lola decides to go and sit in the hotel's garden to reflect on her time there, all that has happened since that day when she accidentally went through the dolmen at Stonehenge and saw the manor house; when she first learned about the Nephilim guard, the moments that have led her to where she is today.

"I thought I would find you here," Josiah says. He is holding two champagne glasses and a bottle of Pol Roger. He hands her a glass and starts to pour.

"Haven't you had enough to drink?" He is swaying slightly, intoxicated from the alcohol he has been consuming throughout the night. He seats himself down next to her.

"Dutch courage, or Polish courage should I say, since we are here?" He shrugs, and sips some of the champagne.

"What do you need courage for?"

Josiah places his glass down onto the floor next to his feet, he takes Lola's from her and does the same. He takes her hands in his.

"Lola," The sound of his voice as he says Lola's name is deeper, more serious than his usual light-hearted tone. The difference in his tone fills her with uncertainty. "Lola," he says again, gentler than before.

"There is something that has been weighing heavily on my chest, my mind, my heart for a while now." Lola senses him debating with himself, wondering the best way to tell her what he is wanting to say.

"Josiah, you know you can tell me anything."

"Lola, when you first decided that you wanted to become a member of the guard, when you first came to stay with us, my initial impression was that you were going to be difficult to work with." *'I did not know exactly what Josiah was wanting to say to me, but I did not expect this';* Lola starts to pull her hands away from his grasp, he pulls them back, not letting them go.

"Not because I thought badly of you. I did not know you well enough to have any preconceived feelings of like or dislike towards you. It was because I thought you were beautiful, I could tell that Atticus did too. We was progressing in our training, I thought the last thing either of one us needed was a distraction. But the more I got to know you, I realised that we needed you, you brought balance to us. Lola, you are the kindest, bravest, most thoughtful, compassionate, strongest, beautiful woman I have ever met, I care about you. We have all noticed the bond that you and Atticus share, and your attraction towards one another. I love Atticus dearly, but he is somebody who has always made decisions using his head. I see that you care for him deeply, I see you would like your relationship to develop into something more. Even though I believe he loves you too, I do not think Atticus thinks,

213

or feels that he can give you more.

"I guess what I am trying to say is that although I know you love Atticus, and he is in love with you too, if Atticus thinks or feels that he cannot give you more, he will follow his head and make the choice not to evolve your relationship with each other. He will do what he thinks is logical, responsible, or the right thing to do in regard with his duty to the guard. Lola, I do not want you to get hurt, so I am asking you, although you love Atticus and want to be with him, I am asking you to not dismiss the other options you have before you."

Lola studies his hands that are still upon hers.

"Is it that obvious? My attraction towards Atticus? I was trying hard not to show it."

"Yes. You are both trying hard to hide it, to fight it; but anyone who is around you when you are together, can feel it."

"I feel foolish."

"You are not foolish, Lola. It would be foolish to care about someone who does not return that affection, but Atticus does. I may be wrong. Maybe Atticus will at some point suggest you acknowledge your affection for each other and pursue it. But I also know Atticus, and he will do what he thinks is right; with what he feels is his duty to the guard, even if it means giving up what his heart truly wants. Promise me Lola that you will consider the other options you have, if other options present themselves?"

I take my hands from under his grip and place mine on top.

"I promise."

*

214

"Lola, a word please."

Lola was so wrapped up in hers and Josiah's conversation she had not noticed Athena approaching them; *'What had he meant about me having other options?'*

"Yes, of course," she shouts over her shoulder towards Athena. Lola smiles at Josiah, he stands up and takes his leave, leaving Athena and Lola alone. Athena takes the place next to her where Josiah had sat.

"Did you and the boys have a good evening?"

"Yes and no."

"Why no?"

"It was just difficult seeing people happy, knowing that would soon change."

"Yes, that is difficult. I remember the first time I had to travel to a time, before a tragedy. The feeling of hopelessness, that there was nothing I could do to help them. Unfortunately, one of the downsides of being part of the guard; not being able to help someone in case it changes the timeline of the lives of everybody else for the worst, running the risk of angering the sky gods. Lola, I was hoping we could talk, talk about Josiah."

"Okay."

"Josiah, Atticus, Markus, and Henri are like my sons. I have noticed that since Josiah's time with the Nazis, he has not been himself, which I can understand why; but I think he is hiding something else from us, something else that he experienced whilst he was there, as well as the torture. Lola, you have become his best friend, if he is going to confide in anyone, he will confide in you. I need you to talk to him before our mission to capture Clotho, because if he is unstable, then his abilities will be too, we cannot afford for anything to go wrong."

"Okay I will talk to him again."

"Thank you. I will suggest that you both have one last training session before we go. How does tomorrow after breakfast sound?"

"Works for me."

*

When Lola arrives in the breakfast room everyone is already there.

"Morning sunshine," Kevin says. Lola cannot help but notice the dark circles under Josiah's eyes have darkened.

"Lola, I was just suggesting that it might be a good idea if you and Josiah had a training session whilst Atticus, Lachesis, Atropos, and I pay a visit to Stefan's office, what do you think?"

"I am up for it if Josiah is?"

"I think that is an excellent idea!" Josiah responds.

"Maybe I should join them instead of going with you?" Atticus suggests.

"Atticus, we need you to come with us. I am sure Lola and Josiah will be fine training alone." Lola gives Atticus a reassuring smile. One of the hotel staff members places a glass of orange juice and a couple of bread rolls in front of her. She breaks the roll; Kevin passes her the jam and butter.

"Where should we go to train?" Lola asks Athena.

"There is a field not far from here that no one ever goes to or passes. Kevin could teleport you there?"

"Of course. It would be my pleasure!" Kevin says.

"Excellent!" Athena says enthusiastically.

*

The field Kevin teleports them to is indeed deserted and in the middle of nowhere.

"I will give you a couple of hours." He winks at Lola, then teleports out leaving them alone.

"So, what's the real reason for Athena wanting us to train?" Josiah blurts out.

"What do you mean?"

"Lola, Athena raised me. I can tell when she is up to something."

Lola exhales and seats herself on the grass; patting a space in front of her instructing Josiah to sit. He seats himself cross-legged in front of her.

"So?" he asks.

"She does think we should train before we collect Clotho tonight, but yes there is another reason. She has asked me to talk to you."

"About?"

"She thinks you are not telling us everything that happened during your time in the Nazi cell, and honestly Josiah I think she is right. My room is right next to yours. I have heard you shouting, crying in your sleep." Josiah uncrosses his legs, and instead spreads them straight out in front of him, he leans back and starts to pick at the grass next to him, avoiding her gaze.

"Josiah?"

"I don't want you to see me as weak."

"Josiah, after everything I have seen you do, trust me when I say, I could never see you as weak. You are one of the strongest men I know, one of the strongest men I have ever met. Nothing you say or do could change my opinion of that.

217

If anything, whatever you decide to share with me will only make me think you are stronger."

"Okay." Josiah re-crosses his legs, Lola places her full attention onto him.

"Have you been told how Atticus, Markus, Henri, and I came to be in Athena and Apollo's care?" Lola nods.

"So, you know about the attack, and the escape passage?" she nods again.

"Okay. So, as you know the cell the Nazis kept me in had stone walls, stone walls that were cold, that were damp."

"Yes."

"Being kept in that cell triggered some memories, memories that I didn't know I had blocked out, until they resurfaced, during my time with the Nazi's. The sound of my mother's screams before Athena, Apollo, and the Nephilim guard that was with them came to our rescue. When the soldier's first broke in, before we were able to reach the passage where Athena and Apollo found us, we hid in the house. Where we hid, I had a clear view of a mirror. I never told anyone this before; but in the reflection of the mirror, I watched as two of the King's men beat, tortured our mother. She saw my face in the reflection, she shook her head, instructing me to stay where I was, and remain quiet. The stone walls of the prison cell brought the memories of the passageway, the screams of the battle that we were leaving behind us, the memory of seeing my mother being beaten, tortured by the King's men in the reflection of the mirror; the fear in her eyes for our lives, for her life, how scared she was, how brave." Josiah closes his eyes tightly, then opens them.

"Since then, every time I close my eyes, I see the image of her being beaten, the fear in her eyes as she saw me watching, watching as the king's men continued to beat her, continued to torture her. Every time I fall asleep, I have these nightmares, I am a child, frozen to the spot, helpless, and unable to help her as she is being beaten, being tortured."

Lola notices a tear start to roll down his cheek. She pulls herself to her knees and wraps her arms around him, embracing him, his head resting on her chest. He wipes the tears from his cheeks away, pulls himself away from her embrace. When you become close to someone, once you have gotten to know someone, you learn when it's best to either talk to them in a moment of hardship, or if it is best to not say anything; in this moment Lola knew that this was a time where it would be best to remain silent.

Josiah finishes pulling himself out from her embrace, stands and holds out his hand to her.

"Let's train!" Lola takes his hand. He pulls her to her feet, she dusts herself off.

"Where would you like to start?" he asks.

"I think we should warm up before anything; laps?" Josiah points to a tree at the edge of the field.

"There and back times ten?" Lola crouches down into the start of a race position.

"On three?" he says.

"One, two, three!" Lola watches him as he takes the lead immediately. Josiah is the fastest man Lola knew when it comes to running. She pushes herself to go faster, she starts to feel the air whooshing past her, the adrenalin starting to pump through her. She feels an electric bolt shoot through her, she feels as if she is flying. She looks to the side of her, at the trees that surround the field, but all she sees is a blur, she stops as she passes another blur, but it wasn't a blur, it was Josiah.

Suddenly she loses her balance, as she stops, she falls over. Lola turns to sit on her bum, Josiah comes to a stop in front of her and offers her his hand, a look of astonishment upon his face.

"Woah! What was that?"

*

When Athena, Atticus, Lachesis, and Atropos arrive at the building where Stefan Zgrzembski worked, they are disappointed to discover that he has already finished work for the day. However, a fellow colleague of his; a lanky copper haired, freckle faced man named Earnest informs them that he is going to see Stefan later that night, as he is going to his and his wife's, for dinner. He asks them if he can pass on a message, which they think best not to.

As they exit the building Kevin is leaning against a wall waiting for them.

"Any luck?"

"No. He has already finished work, but a colleague of his named Earnest, a tall red-haired gentleman with freckles, informed us that Stefan will be joining him and his wife for dinner later tonight. I need you to wait here until he finishes work and follow him home. Once you know where he lives, I need you to teleport us all there."

"Whatever you need me to do. How will I know which red-haired man to follow?"

"As far as I could see, he is the only red-haired man working there. You should have no problem recognising him when he leaves the building." Athena looks up and down the street.

220

"I know where the hotel is from here. We need to go back and inform Josiah and Lola of our plan. Will you be okay?" Kevin nods.

"Okay." Athena hugs Kevin goodbye and she, Lachesis, Atropos, and Atticus walk back to the hotel.

When they arrive back at the hotel, Athena makes her way to Lola's room and knocks. Lola answers the door and invites her in.

"How did it go with Josiah?"

"You were right. More did happen in that cell than he originally told us. But I'm sorry Athena; I cannot tell you what he told me. It's something that only he can tell you, but I think confiding in me has helped him."

"Okay. Do you think he will be well enough to be part of tonight's mission?"

"I believe so."

"And what about you?"

"I am more than okay," Lola answers, Athena smiles.

"There are some minor things Lachesis, Atropos and I still need to discuss before tonight's mission." Athena looks at her watch.

"I am holding the final meeting in an hour, in the courtyard."

Lola nods in understanding.

*

Lola is the first to arrive in the courtyard. Athena, Lachesis, Atropos are next, then Kevin, Atticus, and Josiah. Once they are all there Athena begins informing them of the final plan.

"Listen up." They all take a step closer to each other

221

making a small circle.

"We cannot take our suitcases with us when we go and collect Clotho, so the first thing that's going to happen is that Kevin is going to teleport our suitcases to Earthen Long Barrows, ready for when we travel back to 2049. Whilst we have been here in 1939 Apollo has been working on connecting Pentre Ifan to Earthen Long Barrows, so when we walk through, we are able to travel straight back to Pentre Ifan. As long as we all think about Pentre Ifan and the date August eighteenth, 2049, as we walk through, we should all end up there at the same time. Understand?" They all nod, Athena continues.

"Atticus and Josiah will be the ones to walk through with Clotho. We are going to attach this to her." Athena shows them a piece of equipment that looks similar to a communicator, but with fewer buttons.

"This will connect Clotho's energy to Atticus, and Josiah's energy, camouflaging her own; when she passes through with them, the dolmen will only recognise Atticus and Josiah's energy and where they are wanting to travel to. Once Kevin has teleported our luggage to the dolmen, he will then come back and teleport us to near Clotho's location. When we arrive, Lachesis, and Atropos will be able to sense exactly where Clotho is, from the moment we arrive at the location we will follow them to where she is, Atticus and Josiah will then place the cuff on her, connecting her energy to their own. Kevin will teleport Lola and I first, so when Atticus and Josiah arrive with Clotho, they will have us as back up. Once Lachesis and Atropos have spoken to Stefan, Kevin will teleport them to join us. When we are all reunited, we will then pass through the dolmen together. Any questions?" They all shake our heads

"Great! Meet back here in an hour with your cases."

*

The hour passes by speedily. Whilst waiting for Kevin to teleport their cases to Earthen Long Barrows, Lola finds herself reflecting on her experience in 1939 once more. In some ways it's been as been as exciting, and educational as Lola thought it was going to be. In other ways it made her realise just how lucky she was to not have lived during that time. The times were harder, scarier than she thought they were, she often wondered if she would have been strong enough, brave enough to survive, if this had been the time, she was born into, and grew up in. Her experience made her thankful of how far they had come in a lot of ways; although the Nephilim in her time, are still amidst a time of conflict, with everything that is happening with the S.G.E.; it feels minor in comparison to what these Jewish and Polish people were about to experience with the torture of the Nazis. Athena brings Lola out of her contemplative state.

"Ready?" she says to her.

"More than ready." Kevin holds out his arm for Lola to take. Lola looks up at the building that Kevin has teleported them all too, it looks like it could collapse any moment, she hears the popping teleportation sound of Athena's arrival.

"Is this it?" Athena asks Kevin.

"No. Follow me," he answers.

223

Chapter Fifteen

The group follow Kevin, he leads them to a tall, white building.

"Stefan's colleague lives here?" Lola says looking up at the tall, white structure. It looks no more stable than the one they had been teleported to, originally. As they enter through the main door leaving Kevin outside, they all look up at the wooden staircase running up through the apartment block. It is clear that the walls that were once painted white have greyed with age. They have damp stains and running cracks all over them. Lachesis, and Atropos take the lead, they follow them up slowly, the stairs creaking, they stop outside a wooden door, Lachesis, and Atropos nod. Athena knocks.

*

Moments later the door opens, revealing a mousy-haired lady; the lady is Lena, Irena's friend; she is wearing a navy tea dress and strands of her mousy coloured hair have come loose from her braid, framing her small heart shaped face. In her arms she is cradling a baby.

"Can I help you?" she asks them. Athena takes the lead.

"We believe our friend Celestyna is here, there has been an emergency, we must speak to her immediately."

There is a commotion within the apartment, they push past

Lena, taking her by surprise. Atticus, Lola, and Josiah pull out their weapons, weapons Lena has never seen before, weapons that fill her with fear. The group force themselves further into Lena's home, towards the commotion they had heard.

As they enter the dining area, they find Celestyna standing, holding Stefan at gun point. Irena and Earnest are frozen to their seats.

"Clotho, let him go!" Atropos shouts.

"You're the people from earlier," Earnest says in surprise when he sees them.

Stefan's voice is heard.

"Clotho? You said your name was Celestyna."

Celestyna's body starts to shimmer then glimmer, once the glimmer fades an older lady with jet black, greying hair and leather-like olive skin stands in the place of the young, strawberry blonde, marble-skinned woman that had stood there previously. Gasps escape Irena, Earnest, and Lena's mouths; Stefan tries to take a glimpse at Clotho from the corner of his eye. The gun speeds out of her hand, landing in Atticus's hand instead; Josiah looks at his brother's hand in astonishment.

"Telumkinesis?" Josiah asks, glancing at his brother, impressed. Atticus looks at his brother.

"A recent addition." Suddenly a sharp knife wrapped in vines fly's by Josiah's face, landing in the wall, just scraping his face .

Taking advantage of the sudden distraction lead by Atticus and Lola's moves, Stefan grabs Clotho's arm, twists it behind Her, pinning it behind her back.

"Explain," he demands.

Irena, Lena, and Earnest are looking between Stefan,

Clotho, and the strangers who had just bombarded into the apartment. Irena speaks up, her voice shaking, filled with tones of shock and fear.

"Can somebody please explain to us what is going on? Who you people are?" Irena demands.

Athena replies.

"It does not matter who we are, all you need to know is that we are here to take her back to where she belongs, before any further damage is caused." Athena replies and nods at Atticus and Josiah; a manriki-gusari; an ancient Japanese weapon consisting of a chain with weights attached to either end of it appear around Clotho's wrists. However, the one that had appeared around Clotho's wrists had been created by Hephaestus. It had been created so that either end meet, and connect creating an unbreakable chain; well, until the god or Nephilim that had placed them there, unlocks it. They take her from Stefan and strap a cuff to her wrist, as an extra safety precaution.

"So, what about the real Celestyna?" Stefan asks her.

"Where is she? Filip?"

An evil grin spreads across her wrinkled, old face.

"Dead….just like Filip," she says sneering.

Atropos and Lachesis nod at Athena. Lola, Josiah, Atticus, and Athena escort Clotho out of the apartment. Atropos looks at Irena, Stefan, Lena, and Earnest.

"Irena, Stefan, Lena, Earnest, we are sorry our sister has caused these harrowing events. We hope that you will accept our sincerest apologies and we will ensure that Clotho will be punished accordingly. Stefan, can we please have a word with you in private?" Lachesis nods in the direction of outside the dining area. Stefan follows them.

226

As planned, Kevin is waiting for them outside of the apartment block. He teleports them all to Earthen Long Barrows. Lola notice's that Athena is suffering saying goodbye to him. She thinks back to what Atticus had said about Athena almost marrying a Polish man in the 1930s. Watching them saying their goodbyes pained her, witnessing this intimate moment between them confirms that Kevin was that man. A feeling of loss and regret spread throughout her, poor Athena.

*

As they arrive back at Pentre Ifan, they can hear screams and shouting coming from inside the manor. Using her telepathy, Athena attempts to reach out to her brother Apollo, whom she had left in charge of the manor during her absence.

"Apollo, what is happening?" Silence. She tries Markus. "Markus?" Silence again.

"Henri?" *Silence*

"Apollo?"

"Athena, we are under attack from the S.G.E." Apollo finally replies.

Athena informs her comrades.

"The S.G.E." Suddenly, flames appear, surrounding them. They drop their suitcases to protect their faces from the blaze of the fire.

"It appears, Athena, that you are all in a bit of a predicament. You have two choices Athena, for you know I am the only one able to extinguish the Aionia Floga; release me, save your guard members, my sisters, and go to your brothers and the manors rescue. Or risk us all going through the fire and transporting us all to Hades for infinity." Clotho looks between Lola and Atticus.

"Which you both know is a fate worse than death." directing the comment towards them. The comment confuses Atticus, Lola, and Josiah. All of the groups attention is on Athena; Athena looks at the manor and attempts to contact Apollo.

"Tut, tut Athena you know better than that, no powers can actively break through Aionia Floga."

"I thought the manriki-gusari made her abilities dormant!?" Josiah comments.

"It does, but this is caused by magic, *not* any ability!" Atropos exclaims. A cackle escapes Clotho's mouth. "Clotho, I promise you, if you attempt your little crusade again, we will hunt you down, and make your life as if you *were* eternally stranded in Hades. Let her go!" Athena demands. The manriki-kusari and cuff vanishes from around Clotho's wrists, the Aionia Floga disappears. Clotho escapes back through the portal. Athena, and her comrades rush to aid Apollo and the guards in the battle.

"Apollo, we are coming," Athena telepathically informs him.

Atticus, Josiah, and Lola call for their weapons, the Moirai call for their tapestries of fate.

As they make their way through the knocked down front door of the manor, they follow the sounds of screams. Dashing down the corridor they come across the first victims, some Nephilim, and some wounded members of the S.G.E. Athena, Lola, Josiah, and Atticus continue forwards towards the main battle whilst Lachesis, and Atropos stay behind, adjusting their tapestries to help save the alive, but seriously wounded Nephilim. Once Atropos and Lachesis are sure the wounded Nephilim are healed, they make their way to the balcony that overlooks the dining hall, where the main battle is taking place.

Athena, Atticus, Josiah, and Lola activate their weapons. Josiah punches the floor with his golden knuckle duster causing the ground beneath them to crack. Working as a team, Lola sees the cracks and calls upon the roots below them to wrap around the S.G.E. soldiers legs and pulling their weapons from them, Atticus starts to shoot his arrows.

A man dressed in black cargo trousers, a long sleeved, black top—with a red strap around his arm with the S.G.E. logo on it—charges at Lola with his sword held high. Lola snatches the sword from him by using one of the roots. A woman steps in to assist him, Lola is stopped in her tracks, the woman was a woman Lola knew well.

"Mum?"

The woman pauses, her sword still raised in attack mode.

"Lola." The woman: Lola's mum, on seeing her daughter turns around and runs towards the exit, abandoning her comrade.

Distracted by the sudden shock of seeing her mum—her mum that was supposed to be dead—the soldier embraces the opportunity to attack Lola once more. Out of nowhere, the soldier is suddenly being punched by Josiah. The familiar voice of her mum, Katrine starts to boom out over the battle.

"Soldiers withdraw! Soldiers withdraw! Soldiers withdraw!" The S.G.E. soldiers obey their orders and start to evacuate the manor. Atticus, Athena, Lachesis, Atropos,

Apollo, Markus, Henri, and the Nephilim guard that are accompanying Apollo, join Lola and Josiah. Athena is the first to speak.

"What happened? Why did they withdraw?" Athena asks, confused by the sudden evacuation of the S.G.E soldiers. Atticus notices the distant look on Lola's face.

"Lola?" Atticus places his hand on Lola's shoulder, bringing her out of the daze. Josiah is next to speak.

"Lola?" Lola looks up at Josiah.

"Who was that woman?" Josiah asks her.

Athena also notice's Lola's dismay.

"What woman?" Athena asks questioningly.

Lola looks at Athena.

"My mum. My mum is alive. I need to see my dad," Lola says dashing towards the hall's exit.

"Atticus stop her from leaving. Tell her we will bring Alastair here," Athena instructs, Atticus nods, and runs after her.

"Markus, would you please ring Alastair? Tell him that Lola has received a shock, we insist he comes to her as soon as possible, that you will go and collect him."

"Of course," Markus nods and dishevelled from the battle, leaves the hall immediately. Athena looks around at her fellow team members.

"I am extremely honoured to have fought alongside you all briefly. I am sure that this is the first battle of many, but I know that we have the skills, the courage, the strength, and the connection with each other to face any further battles and win. I shall inform Zeus of your accomplishments, you will all be rewarded. Now please go, heal, rest. Asclepius will come and attend to you all. Apollo, there is something I need to discuss with you." The Nephilim and gods leave Athena, and Apollo alone.

Apollo follows Athena to her office, Athena locks the door behind them. Apollo takes a seat on the burgundy leather couch.

"I had to release Clotho," Athena informs him.

"What?" he replies anxiously.

"She cast a circle of Aionia Floga around us as we came through the portal. I had no choice. She made a comment to Atticus and Lola about them knowing what it was like to be sent to Hades for eternity. I can assure you they looked baffled by the comment. I don't think Lola linked Clotho's comment to what she had dreamt when she travelled the meadows."

"How are we going to inform father of Clotho's escape? We *have* to tell him," Apollo responds.

"I shall tell him the truth; he will understand that I had no choice but to let her go free. The sisters have an empathic connection, we can still keep track of Clotho through them." Athena collapses onto the couch next to her brother.

"Poor Lola, discovering that Katrine is still alive like that."

"She would have found out sooner or later about her mother's betrayal," Apollo responds.

"But by crossing her in battle? The sooner Alastair arrives, the better."

*

Lola is lying on her bed, staring up at the ceiling thinking, about the day's unprecedented events, when she's drawn back to her surroundings by a knocking on her bedroom door. She

231

dazedly walks over to the door and opens it, standing in front of her is her father and Athena. Lola flings her arms around him. They follow her back into her bedroom, they all take a seat on her bed.

"You're looking well. You look strong." Alastair smiles comforting his daughter before continuing.

"Athena has informed me that you came across your mother during the battle. You must have a lot of questions; Athena and I will answer them as much as we can."

"Why was I never told the truth? All this time, she has been alive, and I was never told." Lola asks her father frustratingly.

"It was a difficult circumstance, we had every intention of telling you, when we thought the time was right, when we felt you were ready."

"When was that going to be?"

Athena enters the conversation.

"We were going to tell you, when we had arrived back from Warsaw, when Clotho had been dealt with. You know we are amidst a war with the S.G.E. We knew eventually we would have to fight, but we did not know it was going to be this soon. We are sorry Lola, we are sorry you had to find out this way, I cannot imagine how you must be feeling right now." Lola looks at her father.

"Why? Why did she choose them over us?"

"She believes that we, the Nephilim should be monitored, controlled. That not all Nephilim should be activated, instead only activated if they pass a certain criteria. A criteria based on family history. Her friend Amita: Amita's family had a background of being outlaws, thieves, murderers. Katrine always believed that we were able to choose our paths, no matter our family's history and Amita was proof of this. Amita was the kindest, most generous, loving person she had ever met; she thought there was not a bad bone in her. But then when Amita's abilities started to strengthen, Katrine started to notice changes within her; changes such as the craving for more abilities, more power, the stronger she became, the more she wanted, it was never enough. One night when Amita and Katrine were out on one of their ladies' nights, they were approached by a gang. Your mother begged Amita to just do what the gang wanted; money was not worth getting themselves killed over. Amita laughed at your mother and told her that she was tired of obeying the rules and Amita killed the gang members. That was when she decided that the S.G.E. were right about monitoring which Nephilim should be activated, that we should be controlled."

"Maybe she was right?" Lola shrugs her shoulders.

"Maybe our genetics leave us no choice, as to what paths we end up taking."

"Lola, everybody is born with both light and dark in them, never all dark, or all light. We are all born with free will, with the choice of how we act, react, how we feel. I have discovered what you believe, is what you create. Your mother's friend knew she came from parents who made far more darker choices, than light. She may have believed that because of that, she felt that she too, at some point, was going to do the same. Amita chose fear over love, but she could have chosen love. There is a story of two brothers, whose father chose to take on many lovers, even though he was married to their mother. One brother decided to do the same to his wife, the other brother did not. When their wives asked them why, the brother who chose to follow the same path as his father said; 'Because my father showed me that's what we do'. The second brother when asked the same question answered, 'Because my father showed me what not to do. We always have a choice, Lola." Lola sighs and looks at Alastair.

"Dad, I love you, but I need some time; can we continue this tomorrow?"

"Of course." Alastair kisses Lola on the head. Athena and Alastair leave Lola alone with her thoughts.

*

Atticus and Josiah are laying on their beds when Berty knocks on their door, Atticus answers it.

"A young lady has arrived at the manor wishing to see you sir, she says her name is Adelice," he says to Atticus. Josiah sits up on his bed and joins Atticus at their door.

"Are you sure she said Adelice?" Atticus asks Berty.

"I am certain of it. The lady said you would know who she was. You seem displeased, would you like me to send her away?" Berty asks Atticus.

"No Berty, thank you. Please tell her I shall be down shortly, and please call for Athena. Tell her, myself and my guest shall join her in her office." Atticus shuts the door and walks towards his wardrobe, pulling off his night shirt.

"Adelice? Atticus do you think it is truly her?"

Atticus buttons up the shirt he has pulled from his wardrobe.

"I don't know. If it is, I don't know how she found me, or why she is here."

"I would think that would be obvious. Atticus she would have come to fulfil her duty," Josiah comments. Atticus turns to face his brother before exiting the room.

"That arrangement was made when we were children, during a different time and place. We have not seen each other since, and my parents were taken from me. The arrangement cannot still abide?" A tension surrounds Atticus as he looks at his brother to sympathise with his hypothesis, but no words are said by him. Atticus leaves the room and makes his way to the reception room.

*

As Athena and Alastair are exiting Lola's bedroom, Athena is approached by Berty.

"Atticus requires you urgently to meet him in your office."

"Thank you, Berty." Athena turns to face Alastair; he bids her goodnight.

Athena arrives at her office, to find Atticus and Adelice already waiting for her. The last time Atticus saw his childhood friend was the night before their father's death. He and his brothers were not able to say goodbye, because when morning came, they had no choice but to run. Athena enters the office and stops in her tracks when she sees Adelice, *'How was this possible?'* Athena locks the door behind her.

"Athena, this is…"

"Adelice," Athena says, needing no introduction to whom this woman was, it took Atticus by surprise.

"We always keep track on each Nephilim's life, how else did you think we knew where to find you, your brothers, Henri?" Athena looks to Adelice; she cannot help but notice her clothing. Adelice is dressed head to toe in 1930s fashion.

Adelice starts to confess.

"I followed you, I followed you to the portal and then came through it after you. I knew at some point you would have to return to the dolmen Earthen Long Barrows, and so I waited, and then when that man teleported you there, I hid so you couldn't see me. I overheard where you were travelling to and I used this also." Adelice places her hand into her pocket and pulls out a folded piece of paper that appears to have been unfolded and refolded over and over again, it contains a yellow tinge of age. She passes it Atticus, he takes it from her and begins to unfold it, then starts to read it as she continues to explain herself; it was a note he had written to her when they were children.

"I had taken accommodation in one of the Polish villages, when one night, whilst on my way home from a night out, I heard a commotion. A young man had decided to confront some Nazi soldiers. I decided to gain a closer look, I recognised the young man confronting the Nazis immediately, it was Josiah. At first, I could not believe what I was seeing; after all these years, there he was in Poland, in 1939 of all places. I knew where they would be taking the young man, and so I went to see if they would let me see him, to confirm that it was Josiah that I had seen. When it was confirmed that it was Josiah I had seen, I visited him, and then I asked about you." Adelice looks at Atticus.

"I realised that I had finally found my dear friend, I had to find where you were, and so I tracked you down and started to follow you."

"But what were you doing in 1939? The last time I saw you, you were in France, you were twelve, in 1566!"

"As you know my mother and father were both Nephilim,

just like yours. What you never knew is that my mother did not come from that time."

Athena interrupts Adelice before she finish's her sentence.

"She was born in the 1920s, in Poland, of course, I had forgotten."

Adelice nods and continues.

"My mother died whilst giving birth to me. I was curious as to what she was like. When my abilities kicked in, my father told me the truth about my mother, he trained me, he told me about the portals and how they work. Being a child born from two Nephilim," this time Atticus interrupts her.

"You are able to travel."

Adelice nods.

"So, when I turned nineteen, I decided to travel to Poland, I went through Earthen Long Barrows to 1939 to see if I could find her." Adelice spoke directly to Athena.

"I did not tell her who I was, or what I was, or where I was from. I just wanted to have one conversation with her." Adelice turns to face Atticus.

"I was originally planning on returning home the morning after I had seen Josiah, but then I saw him, and then I found out you were there also. I continued to follow you, and then using the letter you wrote me when you were a child, and a tracking spell, it helped me follow you through the Earthen Long Barrows dolmen." Adelice took Atticus's hands in hers; he looks down at her tiny hands in his, then at her face. His dear friend, his arranged wife to be, has blossomed into a beautiful woman, he cannot deny that; and when she takes his hands in hers, he feels a familiarity, which fills him with warmth and fond memories from when they were children.

"Atticus, my dear friend. I have never forgotten about the

237

arrangement our parents had made with each other. I know time has passed, which we can never gain back, and I am a stranger to you now. All I ask is that you will remember our fond time together and hope that you will consider keeping to our parent's arrangement. It would mean so much to them, for us to be each other's life companions as planned."

Atticus looks between Adelice and Athena. Athena takes control; she walks over to Adelice and embraces her.

"We are pleased you have found us, and that you are safe. We would be delighted if you would stay with us. I must warn you, your arrival at Pentre Ifan is unexpected, and you have caught us during arduous times, but you are most welcome. Now I shall show you to your room, then in the morning we will introduce you to the rest of the manor."

When Atticus enters his and Josiah's bedroom, he finds Josiah sitting up in his own bed waiting for him.

"Was it her?" he asks Atticus

"It was," Atticus replies.

"But how did she find you?"

"She followed me. She saw us in Poland, and then followed us through the portal."

"Did she say why she was here?"

Atticus looks at his brother.

"She hopes that our arrangement will continue."

Josiah feels a mixture of relief and guilt in the pit of his stomach.

"What about Lola?" Josiah asks.

"What about Lola?" Atticus replies.

"It's clear to us all at the manor that you have developed more than platonic friendship feelings for her."

Atticus looks at his brother.

238

"I consider Lola a good friend. I have always known that my duty was, is, to another, and that at some point, our ancestors would find a way to ensure that I will have to fulfil that duty."

"But Atticus, you love Lola. Surely you cannot be considering keeping to the arrangement our parents made?"

"It has always been made clear that when you choose to become a member of the guard, the guard comes first, we must do what the elders request. Our parents arranged our union. Out of duty to the guard, to our elders request. I don't see that I have another choice but to keep the arrangement, despite what my heart wants."

"You cannot be serious? You cannot just dismiss Lola like this. It will break her heart."

"She is a member of the guard, she will understand."

"Again, you cannot be serious?"

Atticus changes back into his night shirt and climbs back into his bed. His back facing Josiah, and switches off his bedside lamp, ignoring Josiah's comment, ending their conversation.

*

In the middle of Lola brushing her long auburn hair, Berty knocks on her door.

"Enter." Berty enters the room.

"Morning Berty."

"Morning, we are all required to attend an emergency meeting in the dining room."

"Thank you, Berty." Berty nods and exits the room.

When Lola enters the dining room, the rest of the manor

239

are already there, plus a young slim woman with dark brown wavy hair, dark penetrating eyes, who seems overjoyed to be there. Her smile is naturally friendly, and pleasantly big. Lola also notices that she is standing rather close to Atticus. As Lola enters the room, she can feel Josiah, Henri, and Apollo watching her like a hawk, whilst Atticus it appears, is trying to avoid looking at her as much as possible. Lola feels an unsettling feeling consume her.

"Ah good, Lola," Athena says.

"Everybody, last night we received an unexpected guest, everyone this is Adelice."

Lola looks straight at Atticus's face; he is determined to not look at her, to not make any eye contact. Remembering her and Josiah's conversation in the hotel garden in 1939, Atticus's conversation with Alex in the air station in Poland, she looks at Josiah who has clearly been watching her, waiting to see her reaction. It explains why Adelice is standing so close to him. Athena continues.

"Adelice will be staying with us from now on. It is also with great congratulations to announce that Atticus and Adelice are engaged." Lola thinks she is going to be sick. *'Atticus is to going to marry her? But they are both far too young to make such a commitment?'* Lola snaps out of her thoughts, paying close attention to Athena.

"We are not sure yet when this will happen, due to present circumstances. Atticus, Adelice, and myself have decided it would be best to wait until the matter of the S.G.E. has been settled. We hope," Athena looks over at Lola,

"We hope that you will all welcome Adelice with open arms. That is all, breakfast will now be served." Lola takes a seat at the table.

During breakfast she catches Atticus's eyes, he immediately looks down, she looks at Josiah, who gives her a friendly smile and holds up his glass of orange juice to her; to which she reacts by doing the same. She feels like she has been thumped in her gut, and her heart and soul have been ripped out.

*

Warsaw, 1942

Irena is walking through the ghetto; she hears Stefan's voice.

"Irena!" Stefan embraces Irena.

"Follow me." Stefan takes Irena by her hand and leads her to a dead-end alley way. Resting against the brick wall is a wheelbarrow with four big wheels.

"Irena, remember when those strangers came and took that woman away at Lena's?"

"How could I forget."

"Do you remember when those ladies wanted to speak to me in private?" Irena nods.

"I never told you what they told me; because they told me not to tell you, not until this day. They insisted. They said if I disobeyed them that there would be great consequences." Stefan pulls aside the wheelbarrow to reveal a vent of some sort. He pulls off the gate, climbs in and asks Irena to follow him. He pulls the wheelbarrow back to hide the hole in the wall and places the gate back up. He switches on a flashlight and starts to walk through an underground tunnel. Irena follows him.

"Stefan, where are we? Where are we going?" He stops at the shelter that he has built; inside the shelter are beds, and

241

trunks of clothes. Irena looks around.

"Where are we?"

"We are in an underground tunnel. This tunnel connects to other tunnels all over Warsaw and the outskirts."

"Why are you showing me this?"

"Irena, this is your destiny."

"I don't understand."

"You were saying you wish you could help the children escape the ghetto. Those women, they told me about this place, this tunnel. You must use these tunnels to help sneak those children out. The strange women told me that you must not doubt yourself, that you are going to help thousands of children and this tunnel will be the start of that."

"But how?"

"With help from the resistance, they will provide you with clothes for the children, money, and fake passports so the children are able to take on new identities. The have connections with families, and convents outside of the ghetto. Families and convents who are willing to help hide the children taken to them."

Irena looks around at the shelter, the tunnel, filled with the excitement and the joy of knowing that she will be able to help those innocent Jewish children. She throws her arms around Stefan.